SAMANTHA SANDERSON

WITHOUT A TRACE

CALGARY PUBLIC LIBRARY

JUL 2017

Also by Robin Caroll

Samantha Sanderson at the Movies (Book One)
Samantha Sanderson on the Scene (Book Two)
Samantha Sanderson Off the Record (Book Three)

Other books in the growing Faithgirlz!™ library

Bibles

The Faithgirlz! Bible
NIV Faithgirlz! Backpack Bible

Faithgirlz! Bible Studies

Secret Power of Love
Secret Power of Joy
Secret Power of Goodness
Secret Power of Grace

Fiction

The Good News Shoes

Riley Mae and the Rock Shocker Trek
Riley Mae and the Ready Eddy Rapids
Riley Mae and the Sole Fire Safari

From Sadie's Sketchbook

Shades of Truth (Book One)
Flickering Hope (Book Two)
Waves of Light (Book Three)
Brilliant Hues (Book Four)

Sophie's World Series

Meet Sophie (Book One)
Sophie Steps Up (Book Two)
Sophie and Friends (Book Three)
Sophie's Friendship Fiasco (Book Four)
Sophie Flakes Out (Book Five)
Sophie's Drama (Book Six)

The Lucy Series

Lucy Doesn't Wear Pink (Book One)

Lucy Out of Bounds (Book Two)

Lucy's Perfect Summer (Book Three)

Lucy Finds Her Way (Book Four)

The Girls of Harbor View

Girl Power (Book One)

Take Charge (Book Two)

Raising Faith (Book Three)

Secret Admirer (Book Four)

Boarding School Mysteries

Vanished (Book One)

Betrayed (Book Two)

Burned (Book Three)

Poisoned (Book Four)

Nonfiction

Faithgirlz Handbook

Faithgirlz Journal

Food, Faith, and Fun! Faithgirlz Cookbook

Real Girls of the Bible

My Beautiful Daughter

You! A Christian Girl's Guide to Growing Up

Girl Politics

Everybody Tells Me to Be Myself, but I Don't Know Who I Am

Devotions for Girls Series

No Boys Allowed

What's a Girl to Do?

Girlz Rock

Chick Chat

Shine on, Girl!

The Beauty of Believing

Check out www.faithgirlz.com

SAMANTHA SANDERSON

WITHOUT A TRACE

BOOK FOUR

ROBIN CAROLL MILLER

ZONDERKIDZ

Without a Trace
Copyright © 2016 by Robin Caroll Miller

Requests for information should be addressed to:

Zonderkidz, 3900 *Sparks Dr. SE, Grand Rapids, Michigan 49546*

ISBN 978-0-310-74251-7

All Scripture quotations, unless otherwise indicated, are taken from The Holy Bible, *New International Version®, NIV®*. Copyright © 1973, 1978, 1984, 2011 by Biblica, Inc.® Used by permission. All rights reserved worldwide.

Any Internet addresses (websites, blogs, etc.) and telephone numbers in this book are offered as a resource. They are not intended in any way to be or imply an endorsement by Zondervan, nor does Zondervan vouch for the content of these sites and numbers for the life of this book.

All rights reserved. No part of this publication may be reproduced, stored in a retrieval system, or transmitted in any form or by any means—electronic, mechanical, photocopy, recording, or any other—except for brief quotations in printed reviews, without the prior permission of the publisher.

Zonderkidz is a trademark of Zondervan.

Cover design: Kris Nelson
Interior design: Denise Froehlich

Printed in the United States of America

---

15 16 17 18 19 20 /DCI/ 20 19 18 17 16 15 14 13 12 11 10 9 8 7 6 5 4 3 2 1

For Gracelyn . . .
Love you sweet girl,
Aunt Robin

CHAPTER ONE

"Why can't spring break hurry up and get here already?" Samantha "Sam" Sanderson whined to her bestie as she shut her locker in the breezeway of the seventh grade ramp of Joe T. Robinson Middle School.

The storm that had passed through just an hour or so ago had left the walkways wet, but the air cooler.

Makayla Anderson wrinkled her nose at Sam. "You're just excited because you get to go on a cruise for spring break."

"Yeah, and leave the rest of us here to be jealous," Lana Wilson said as she joined them at the lockers.

"I thought you were going camping with your parents for spring break." Sam slung her backpack over her shoulder and stared at Lana. Her parents had divorced, gone through counseling, then recently remarried. They were starting to do things as a family again, and Lana looked happier than Sam had ever seen her.

Lana shut her locker and stared at Sam. "Yeah, but camping here in the natural state isn't quite the same as going on a cruise and getting to swim with the dolphins. Hello? Did you not go through the same tornado warning I did?"

"She's got you there, Sam," Makayla said. "Arkansas or the Caribbean . . . such a tough choice."

Sam laughed. "Hey, it's the first real vacation we've had in years. Mom or Dad are always working, or something else comes up." Sam's dad was a detective with the Little Rock Police Department and her mom was an award-winning investigative journalist.

"I know. We're only teasing." Makayla nudged Sam. "I'd better run to the bus or I'll be stuck sitting with the sixth graders."

"Me, too," Lana said. "I heard some of the sixth graders were crying because of the weather and the safety procedures."

"It was a little scary," Makayla confessed.

"Oh, man. I forgot the flyers," Sam said, rolling her eyes. "I told Ms. Pape I'd put them in the teachers' boxes before I left."

"Call me later then." Makayla smiled, then rushed off toward the circle of school buses, Lana with her. "Happy hump day!"

Sam hitched the backpack up on her shoulder and

headed back into the school newspaper classroom. Ms. Pape had already left, but the paper's editor, and Sam's nemesis, Aubrey Damas, was still in the room.

"What are you doing back here, *Samantha*?" Aubrey never failed to use Sam's full name, just because she knew Sam hated it.

Eighth grader Aubrey was Sam's editor and she went out of her way, attempting to make Sam miserable. It was as if Aubrey took it personally that Sam wanted to be the best journalist in the history of the school, then high school, then college, then be as award-winning as her mom. After all, she had her heart set on attending the University of Missouri, which was ranked as the number one journalism college by Princeton Review.

For the past three years, two students from Robinson High School had received full scholarships from Mizzou, and Sam aspired to do the same—especially since her parents had made it abundantly clear that hard work was the key to success. But getting on the high school paper was quite the task. As a general rule, they didn't allow freshmen on staff . . . except for the editor of the middle school's paper. That one freshman, they would allow on without question. Sam was determined to make editor next year.

But first, she had to make it past Aubrey Damas this year.

"Just getting the ad flyers to put in the teachers'

boxes." Sam grabbed the stack off the edge of the big layout table. "What are you still doing here?"

"Not that it's any of your business," Aubrey said, flipping her hair over her shoulder, "but I'm working on the new layout design."

The paper had recently received a rather large donation, which the staff had voted to use to redesign the look of the paper.

Sam swallowed a sigh and forced a smile. "Would you like any help?" she offered.

Aubrey snorted. "From you? I don't think so."

"Suit yourself." Sam turned and headed to the office. She was determined not to let Aubrey get under her skin so much, even though Aubrey seemed to thrive on getting on Sam's last nerve.

The school secretary looked up as Sam entered the office. "What can I do for you, Sam?" Mrs. Darrington asked. A few gray hairs had escaped her bun and her glasses had slipped down the bridge of her nose. "We're about to close up here."

Sam held up the flyers. "I just need to put these in the teachers' boxes for tomorrow."

The secretary lumbered toward her. "What are they?"

Sam passed one to her. "It's the paper's notification of selling ads for upcoming editions. It has the specs and the prices and everything. Ms. Pape will make the announcement in the morning, but wanted the teachers to have the flyers to hand out to the students."

Mrs. Darrington handed back the paper. "Go ahead then."

Sam eased behind the counter, set her backpack on the desk, and moved to the message area, where all the teachers had their slots, and began sticking the binder-set stacks in each bin. Only two more weeks and three days of school, then she'd be on her first cruise ship. Boy, was she ever excited! Their only planned excursion was to swim with dolphins and Sam could hardly wait.

The door to the office squeaked open. Sam moved to look around the wall. A small, dark-haired woman stepped inside, her eyes wide and face flushed.

"I can't find my son," a woman said, clearly on the verge of tears.

Mrs. Darrington shot to her feet. "Who is your son, ma'am?"

Sam shifted, staring at the lady.

"Tam Lee."

"Tam wasn't in last period, Mrs. Lee," Sam blurted out. She clamped her hand over her mouth as Mrs. Darrington pinned her with a glare.

"He wasn't?" Mrs. Lee asked Sam.

"You're positive he was at school today, Mrs. Lee?" Mrs. Darrington asked as she threw Sam a *keep-your-mouth-shut* look and sat back down behind her desk and accessed her computer.

Tam's mother focused on the secretary. "Yes. I

dropped him off myself this morning. Seven fifty on the dot."

Sam leaned against the wall, forcing herself to be silent. Tam hadn't been in newspaper last period, that much was for sure. Sam had been at school since eight, and she hadn't seen Tam in the cafeteria where all students had to remain until the bell rang. It was *possible* she just didn't see him—she'd been talking to Makayla and Felicia about the cruise and not paying attention to everyone else around—but Tam usually spoke to her.

"I'm showing he was marked absent for every class today," Mrs. Darrington said, standing up behind her desk.

"But I dropped him off here myself." Mrs. Lee's voice rose and her face got paler.

Mrs. Darrington turned to Sam. "Please go get Mrs. Trees."

Sam nodded and rushed down the office's hallway. It was a rare thing for her to be in a hurry to go to the principal's office since going there usually meant she was in hot water—but not today. Not now. She was worried about Tam. Where was he?

Mrs. Trees had her keys in her hand and her purse on her shoulder as Sam barged into her office. "What is it, Sam?"

"Mrs. Darrington needs you. Tam Lee's mother is here and Tam is missing."

The principal dropped her keys and purse onto her

desk and hurried to the front office. Sam kept at her heels, but quietly. The last thing she needed to do was draw attention to herself and be sent away. She moved to the backside of the office, where she'd been putting the flyers in the teachers' boxes.

Mrs. Darrington quickly explained the situation to Mrs. Trees in hushed tones.

"I'm positive I dropped him off at exactly seven fifty. I know because I checked the time when I saw the gate wasn't unlocked and I was worried I might be too early," Mrs. Lee said. "I remember thinking that you were late unlocking the gate and that I might need to call the office again."

Sam bit her lip as she eavesdropped. Mrs. Lee had touched on something that annoyed Sam's dad too. Students were not supposed to be dropped off before seven forty-five. The school didn't unlock the gate so kids could enter by the cafeteria until that time. However, there were many times the security guard didn't unlock the gate until closer to eight, or sometimes even after. Dad had complained several times about buses letting students off with the gate still locked, and that there was no place for the students to safely wait. Sam had always thought Dad was just in "cop mode" when he complained, but maybe he'd been right.

"I'll check with my staff to see exactly what time the gate was unlocked this morning, but is it possible that

Tam skipped school and is now at home waiting for you?" Mrs. Trees asked.

"No. My son doesn't skip school." Mrs. Lee's voice sounded confident. "He never has. He doesn't have a reason to. He's a wonderful student."

Sam silently agreed from behind the wall. Tam was one of the smartest kids she knew, and he loved school. He always had a smile and was willing to help anyone, even the bratty sixth graders.

"Besides," Mrs. Lee said, "I've already called home, just in case. There was no answer. No answer on his cell phone either." Her face turned even redder. "I called his father, and he hasn't heard from Tam since this morning."

"Well, he wasn't marked present in any classes today," Mrs. Darrington said.

"Then something happened to him this morning after I dropped him off. When you didn't have the gates unlocked on time . . ." Mrs. Lee's voice rose again. "I'm calling the police."

Sam peeked around the wall as Mrs. Lee put a cell phone to her ear and began talking. Mrs. Trees looked at Mrs. Darrington. "Get both of the security guards in here, right now."

As Mrs. Darrington rushed to the walkie-talkie, Mrs. Trees spied Sam. "Sam, you need to go now."

Sam put the last of the flyers in the slots. "Yes, ma'am. I'm just about finished."

"Now, Samantha." No question she meant Sam was finished right now.

Sam nodded and swallowed. She grabbed her backpack from the desk, slung it over her shoulder, and moved slowly toward the door.

"The police said they'd send someone over immediately," Mrs. Lee said, sliding her phone back into her purse.

Sam paused at the door. "I hope you find Tam soon. He's my friend," she told Mrs. Lee, then stepped out into the open breezeway.

She bounded down the stairs just as one of the security guards approached, a graveness showing on his face. The buses were already gone, so Sam rushed to the parking lot. She drew up short for just a moment as she spied Dad's truck instead of Mom's car.

"Hey, pumpkin," Dad said. "I was about to come looking for you. How was school?"

She tossed her backpack onto the floorboards of the backseat. "Why isn't Mom picking me up?"

"She's finishing up her last piece before vacation. The power cutting off put her a little behind schedule." Dad reached for the keys in the ignition. "Hop in."

"Dad, the police are on their way here right now."

"Why? What's going on?"

Sam quickly filled him in, then ended with, "Can you please go find out what's going on? I'm scared for Tam."

"It's not my case." But his eyes looked weighted

down in the corners. "The sheriff's office has jurisdiction here."

"Can't you just go in and offer support or something until they get here? Mrs. Lee was really upset." Her own fear for Tam twisted in her stomach. "And Mrs. Trees knows you."

He sighed, then pulled the keys from the ignition. "Just to keep everyone calm until someone from the sheriff's office gets here."

"Thank you, Daddy." Sam slammed the passenger door closed and had to double-step to keep up with her dad's long stride.

As she passed the gate and followed her father into the office, her mind wrapped around one question and one question only: where was Tam?

CHAPTER TWO

Detective Sanderson," Mrs. Trees said as they walked into the office. For once she looked relieved to see him rather than her usual look of annoyance at his presence. Which, to be honest, usually meant Sam had done something questionable.

"I don't mean to interfere, Mrs. Trees. I just thought perhaps I could assist a bit," he said in that calm and steady voice of his. Sam loved that about her dad—he seemed to ooze confidence that made people less likely to panic around him.

"Of course. Detective Sanderson, this is Mrs. Lee." The principal gestured to Tam's mother who sat on the bench across from the front counter.

"I understand you can't find your son," Dad said to Tam's mother in his soothing tone as he eased onto the bench beside her. "I'm not here in an official capacity as this isn't my jurisdiction, but I'm happy to help in any way possible."

Mrs. Lee nodded. "I appreciate that. I can't imagine where Tam is." She started wringing her hands, literally. Sam thought that only happened in movies or books.

Dad noticed too because he laid his hand on top of hers. "Do you have a picture of Tam? The sheriff's office will need a recent picture."

She blinked several times. "On my phone, but I don't have a paper picture." The panic eased back into her voice as she tapped her phone and showed him a photograph.

"It's okay. We can print one off your phone." Dad took her cell phone and handed it to Sam, giving her a nod.

Sam was able to identify the school's printer easily enough and send the picture to print. She handed the phone back to Mrs. Lee, then pulled the picture from the printer. Her heart skipped a beat as Tam smiled up at her. Had he been safe during the bad storm?

She laid the picture on the counter and shifted to stand against the wall on the other side of the counter. Maybe if she stayed out of Mrs. Trees' direct line of sight, the principal wouldn't make her leave or wait somewhere else.

"We've sent the security officers out to look over the campus," Mrs. Trees offered.

The office door opened, and a Pulaski County

sheriff's deputy in a brown uniform filled the space. He was tall, taller than Sam's dad, but a bit heavier. He spoke out of the corner of his mouth from under a droopy moustache. "Someone needs to fill out a missing person's report?" he asked with a voice as thick as his black hair.

Mrs. Lee nodded. "My son. He's missing." She went back to wringing her hands.

"I see." The deputy set his clipboard on the counter.

Dad extended his hand. "Detective Charles Sanderson, LRPD."

"Deputy Orson Jameson." The deputy shook his hand. "Your son?"

"No. I just happened to be here when Mrs. Lee couldn't find her son."

Sam pinched her lips together and tried to blend into the wall beside the counter. *Please don't ask us to leave.*

"I see." The deputy looked at Mrs. Lee. "Tell me what happened." He lifted his pen over his notebook.

"I dropped Tam off at ten before eight this morning. I'm positive about the time because I checked the clock in my car when I saw the gate wasn't unlocked yet." Mrs. Lee threw the principal a hard look. "The gate is supposed to be open at seven forty-five, but it's hardly ever unlocked on time."

"Now, that's not—" Mrs. Trees started.

"We'll get to you in a moment," the deputy

interrupted. He nodded at Tam's mom. "Please, continue. You dropped him off. Did you see where he went, what he did, who he was with? Tell me everything you remember." His tone was much softer when he talked to Tam's mom. Sam liked that.

Mrs. Lee mashed her lips together for a moment. "He got out of the car and walked toward the gate area. There were several other kids sitting on the stairs and bunched around the table there."

"Did he join any of the other kids?" The deputy still held his pen above the notebook.

Mrs. Lee shook her head. "He leaned against the wall, on the side opposite the gate." She looked at Deputy Jameson. "He was alone and gave me a wave as I drove off."

"Did you recognize any of the other kids you saw there?"

"No. I couldn't even tell you how many boys or girls there were."

"That's okay," he said with a smile, his tone very gentle. "What was he wearing today?"

Without pausing, Mrs. Lee replied. "Jeans and his gray t-shirt with SENATORS in gold. He wears black sneakers."

Dad handed Deputy Jameson the picture Sam had printed. "Here's a recent photograph of Tam."

"Thanks." The deputy looked at the picture, then slipped it into his notebook before smiling at Mrs. Lee again. "After he leaned against the wall and waved, what happened?"

She shrugged. "I drove off, just like I always do. I went to work, then came to pick him up like every day. Except he wasn't here. He's gone." Tears filled her eyes.

Sam blinked herself. Tam was a good guy, certainly not one who would make his mom worry like this. Where could he be?

"Have you tried calling his cell phone?" the deputy asked.

Mrs. Lee shook her head. "He leaves his phone at home on the charger. It's one of his dad's rules—no cell phone at school."

The security guards came into the office, filling the already-crowded entryway. "No sign of anyone," Officer Burns told Mrs. Trees. "Only kids out there are the ones who are supposed to be, and are with their coaches."

"Tam was absent from every class today?" Deputy Jameson asked.

Mrs. Darrington nodded. "I've checked the online attendance. The teachers update in the system daily, so the records are accurate. Tam was marked absent in every single class."

Deputy Jameson turned toward Mrs. Trees. "I noticed cameras when I came in. Do you have any pointing at the gate area?"

Mrs. Trees shook her head. "Not yet. We've ordered two more cameras, but they haven't come in."

"Is there a teacher on duty in that area at seven forty-five?" Deputy Jameson asked.

"Not a teacher, but one of the security guards is in the cafeteria after the gate is opened, while the other is in the circle to watch children crossing the bus line."

"What time was the gate unlocked this morning?"

Mrs. Trees looked at Officer Burns. "What time did you unlock the gate?"

He was a massive man, bigger than some of the Razorback football players that Sam had seen at the last game Dad had taken her to. Sam wasn't a big fan of the security guard, though. He could be downright rude to kids if they weren't in certain cliques. Sam's group wasn't included in his favorites.

Officer Burns shrugged. "Usual time, I suppose. Seven forty-five."

Mrs. Lee shook her head. "No, I looked at my clock when I dropped Tam off. It was seven fifty and the gate was still locked."

Mrs. Trees glared at Officer Burns. "Were you late again?"

He nodded, but dropped his gaze to the floor. "I guess I was a little late."

"How late?" Deputy Jameson asked.

"Just a few minutes." He lifted his gaze and crossed his arms over his chest.

"You were already five minutes late when I dropped off Tam," Mrs. Lee said, her voice shaking.

"I usually am on time, but today, traffic was bad and I—"

"There've been a lot of times when the gate hasn't been unlocked on time," Mrs. Lee said. "I've called the office several times to complain."

Officer Burns cut a hard stare at Tam's mom.

"I've called about the same thing myself," Dad reinforced.

"At any rate, apparently the gate was unlocked late today," Mrs. Trees said, throwing Sam's father a hard look.

"I'm trying to determine a timeline," the deputy explained. He looked back at Officer Burns. "As close to accurate as you can be, what time do you think you unlocked the gate?"

The security officer's Adam's apple bobbed up and down. "I was maybe ten minutes or so late."

"Ten to fifteen minutes?" Deputy Jameson pressed.

"Maybe that." The security officer nodded, pulling out his bandana and dabbing at his now sweaty forehead, even though it was cool enough in the office. "And kids can't leave once they come through."

"Okay." The deputy straightened. "So we're looking at a very short timeframe here. Between seven fifty and five after eight, that's when Tam Lee went missing. Fifteen minutes at most."

Sam swallowed. That was a really short time. She tried to remember when she'd been dropped off. It'd been straight up eight, and kids were just going into the cafeteria. Makayla's bus had already dropped her off, so Sam had to run to be able to walk in with Mac. Did she see Tam then? She didn't think so, but wasn't sure. She honestly couldn't remember.

"Do you know if your son would deliberately not go to the designated area?" Deputy Jameson asked.

Mrs. Lee shook her head. "Tam wouldn't do that. He's a rule follower."

The deputy looked at Mrs. Trees and raised a single eyebrow.

"Tam is an honor student here and has never been in trouble," the principal confirmed.

"Has he ever skipped school before?" Deputy Jameson asked.

"No," Mrs. Lee answered before Mrs. Trees could.

Mrs. Darrington typed on her computer. "He's not had an unexcused absence all year." She tapped some more. "Or even the two years before this."

"I see." The deputy scribbled on his notebook, then tapped his chin with the pen. "Mrs. Lee, does your son dabble in drugs or alcohol?"

She gasped. "No, of course not."

Sam pinched her lips together. Drugs or alcohol ... Tam? No way.

"He just has to ask, Mrs. Lee. He's not accusing Tam of anything," Sam's dad said in his soothing tone.

"I understand." But Tam's mom sounded a little shakier than before.

"What about your son's relationships at home?" the deputy continued.

"What about them?" Mrs. Lee locked stares with Deputy Jameson.

"How do you and your son get along? Does his father live in the home?"

"Yes, Tam lives with me and my husband." She shrugged. "We get along like a normal family, I suppose." But she sounded a little unsure, even to Sam.

"How about last night and today even?" Deputy Jameson leaned a little closer to Mrs. Lee. "Did either of you have a disagreement with your son? Ground him? Make him angry?"

She hesitated. "Well, he wanted to go spend the night with a friend last night but we said no." She looked at Sam's dad. "It was a school night and that's against our rules."

Sam's dad nodded. He had the same rule, unless there were special circumstances.

"Was he angry you wouldn't let him go?" the deputy asked.

"A little, I suppose." Mrs. Lee wrung her hands again.

"So it's possible he ran away." The way the deputy said it was more of a statement than a question.

Tam wouldn't run away. He was too mature for that. Sam sucked in air, which drew Deputy Jameson's attention. "And you are?"

"My daughter," Dad said at the same time Sam replied with, "Sam Sanderson."

"Do you know Tam?" the deputy asked her.

She nodded. "He's on the newspaper staff with me, but he wasn't in class today."

"Did you see him at all today?"

She shook her head. "Not that I can remember."

"Deputy," Mrs. Lee interrupted, "just because my son was disappointed that he didn't get his way doesn't mean he ran away. Tam's never run away from home and he wouldn't start now."

The deputy seemed to ignore her statement and moved on. "Who was the friend he wanted to visit?"

"Luke Jensen."

Sam gasped again. Luke Jensen . . . he was . . . well, he was the cutest boy at Robinson Middle School. At least as far as Sam was concerned.

The deputy shot her a hard stare, then glanced at her dad. "I think I've got it from here, Detective."

Oh, no! She'd gotten them the boot.

Her dad stood and pressed a hand on Mrs. Lee's shoulder. "If we can do anything for you, just let us know." He nodded at the deputy and Mrs. Trees. "Come on, Sam."

Now how was she going to find out what they were doing to find Tam?

"Sam?" Dad used that no-room-for-arguments tone he often reserved especially for her.

She let out a breath and moved alongside her father. "I'm sure Tam's okay, Mrs. Lee," she said before following Dad out of the office.

Boy, she sure hoped she was right.

CHAPTER THREE

"Thanks for staying, Dad. I know Mrs. Lee's really worried," Sam said as she and her father climbed into his truck.

He didn't respond until he'd started the engine, put on his seatbelt, and backed out of the parking space. "Sam, if you know anything about where Tam might be, you should tell me."

"Dad, I don't. I promise." She was a little hurt he implied she might. Then again, she had kept things from him in the past. But not about something like this.

"I'm guessing you'll ignore me if I advise you not to go about investigating Tam's disappearance on your own, right?"

"Tam's my friend, Dad. I'm worried about him." That was the honest truth, and friends would try and figure out where he was, to make sure he was okay.

"I know, pumpkin. I just want you to be safe, and stay out of the sheriff's way. Law enforcement doesn't play around when a child is missing."

"Will the FBI get called in?"

He chuckled. "Not unless a ransom demand is received." He cut his eyes over to her. "Is Tam's family extremely wealthy?"

She shrugged. "I dunno." He didn't seem to have more than anybody else at school.

"Is his father or his mom in a position of power at work?"

Sam shrugged again. "I don't think his mom works and his dad is a brain or heart doctor or something." She chewed her bottom lip, thinking. "Do you think he might have been kidnapped?"

"I very seriously doubt it."

"Then where is he, Dad?" Nothing made sense. "Tam isn't the type to ditch school or to run away. He's smart and he's funny. He's an honor student, on the newspaper, and in EAST, just not my class." Environmental And Spatial Technology, EAST, was a class that focused on student-driven service projects by using teamwork and cutting-edge technology, including GPS/GIS mapping tools, architectural and CAD design software, 3D animation suites, virtual reality development, and more.

"You don't really know how people are, Sam. You don't know what someone's home life is like. There are a lot of things people don't share. Especially at your age."

"What's that mean?"

He sighed as he turned into their driveway. "Just that if there's something going on, many times kids in middle school won't talk about their family issues with friends, much less teachers or counselors."

"Like what kinds of stuff going on, Dad?"

Dad turned off the engine and turned to face her. "Like trouble at home. Arguments between parents. Any kind of domestic disturbances. Kids arguing with their parents. Being hit." He shrugged. "Especially boys."

"You think Tam deals with any of that stuff?" She couldn't imagine that being the case. Tam was too sweet, and his mom seemed way too nice, but if what Dad implied was true, who really knew?

"I'm not saying he does, but I'm not ruling out that he doesn't. I'm just saying that in my professional experience, kids your age can surprise you. Don't think you know someone just because you're friends at school." He opened the driver's side door of the truck and stepped to the driveway.

Sam did the same, grabbing her backpack from the backseat and slinging it over her shoulder. She needed to talk to Makayla. Maybe Mac had seen or heard something about Tam.

"Mom texted me that she was running to the post office, then is picking up dinner on her way home," Dad called out as Sam reached down to pet her dog Chewy, that greeted her at the front door.

"Did you miss me, Chewy?" The black and brown German hunt terrier jumped up and down.

Sam laughed and skipped with her dog to the kitchen door. She noticed over half the food bowl was still full. "Did the storms scare you, huh?" She rubbed between the dog's ears. Chewy didn't like storms. She really didn't like the tornado sirens that go off either. Whenever storms were in the area, the dog would hardly eat.

Sam patted the dog's head a final time, let Chewy outside, then headed to her bedroom. She dropped her backpack on the floor and fell across her bed. The ceiling fan spun on low, just enough to move the cool air from the vent in the ceiling around the room and keep the temperature comfortable.

Was Tam comfortable wherever he was?

BabyKitty, the white kitten she'd recently rescued, uncurled from her position at the foot of Sam's bed. She stretched and yawned, then "kneaded" the fleece blanket she thought was hers, and curled back up and closed her eyes.

Sam sat up, smiling and shaking her head at the cat, then dug her phone out of her pocket. She leaned over and ran her fingers through the cat's thick, white fur as she quickly dialed Makayla's cell number.

"Hey, girl. Took you long enough to call," Mac said. Her voice always cheered up Sam, no matter what, because Mac was so happy and upbeat all the time.

Even when her mom was on her case or she was exhausted from karate practice, she was still so cheerful. Today was no exception, even though Sam had a lot of serious stuff on her mind. "I thought maybe you'd gotten in trouble and I wouldn't be able to go home with you tomorrow."

"Tam Lee is missing!" Sam blurted out.

"Missing? What? Tell me."

Sam filled Makayla in on everything that had happened and all that was said, then almost out of breath, added, "I don't remember seeing him this morning at all in the cafeteria or outside the gate. Do you?"

"Hmmm. I don't think so. I don't remember. He usually goes out of his way to say hello to you if he sees you, and that's usually how I see him."

"I know." Sam wormed across her bed until she leaned against the pillows and headboard. She kicked her shoes to the floor. "I can't imagine where he could be." She thought about the storm. Had Tam been okay? Had he been inside where he was protected from all the rain and hail and wind?

"Me either, but I don't know him as well as you do."

Sam thought about what her dad had told her. "Well, maybe I don't know him all that well. I mean, he's nice and we chat in Newspaper and if we see each other in the hall, but I don't really know him, know him."

"I guess. Hey, maybe he's home now."

"That'd be good. Let me call and see." Sam had all

the newspaper staff phone numbers, cell and home. It was the paper's policy. She pulled out the list with all the numbers.

"While you're doing that, I'll do some poking around online and see if I can see anything mentioning him on social media. If he ran away or something, he probably posted something somewhere to let his friends know how to contact him." Unless he didn't want his parents to see. "Or he told someone he'd private message them."

Mac was not only ninja smart with computers, she was scary brilliant when it came to thinking of the obvious.

"I'll call you back." Sam dialed Tam's cell number.

The call was answered on the first ring. "Hi, this is Tam. Leave me a message and I'll call you back."

Sam hung up, a little unnerved with hearing his voice, but knowing he was missing. Maybe not . . . maybe he was at home. She dialed the number listed for his home.

"Hello," Mrs. Lee said, her voice weak over the line.

"Mrs. Lee, this is Sam Sanderson. I met you in the office."

"Yes?"

"I'm wondering if you've found Tam yet." *Please, God, let Tam be home and safe.*

"No." Mrs. Lee sniffed. "The police are here, looking through his room now. They're taking his phone to go through back at the station. Although, I have no idea what they hope to find. He didn't run away, he's missing. They won't listen to me. They don't understand what a good boy my Tam is." Her rambling was evident, even to Sam.

She didn't know what to say to Tam's mother. "I'm sorry. I'm praying for him."

"Thank you, Sam. I need to get off the phone now." Mrs. Lee hung up before Sam could say goodbye.

She quickly called Makayla back. "He's not home," she said as a way of greeting as soon as her bestie answered. "Mrs. Lee said the police are taking his phone to go through it. They're there looking through his room. Don't know why."

"Probably to see if there are any clues about where he could be. That's why they do it on the crime shows."

"Dad says those things are full of baloney." Dad usually ranted about how ninety percent of what was in those television dramas was misleading and had nothing to do with real police work.

"They probably are."

"Did you have any luck?" Sam asked.

"I've checked all his social media sites and he hasn't posted anything since last night. His last post was about being bummed that he couldn't go visit a friend because of his dad's stupid rules, and that wasn't made from his mobile device, so he was most likely posting from his computer."

"He actually posted that his dad's rules are stupid?" Sam was pretty outspoken herself, but she wasn't quite brave enough to publicly post that she thought her dad's rules were stupid. She'd be grounded for sure.

"Yep."

Maybe Dad was right and she didn't really know Tam all that well. Maybe he *had* been angry enough to run away.

"Are you going to write a post for the paper's blog?" Makayla asked.

"I think so. Maybe someone saw him or talked to him or something." Sam couldn't imagine not a single person knowing what happened to him.

"I checked the local news pages. There hasn't been an AMBER Alert issued yet. That's good, right?"

"I don't know." The AMBER Alert Program activated urgent bulletins in many missing children cases. The alert would broadcast on television, Internet, and over cell phones to instantly spur an entire community to assist in the search for a missing child. "From the way the sheriff's deputy acted, I think they're treating this as Tam running away from home. I don't think they put out AMBER Alerts for suspected runaways."

"After reading his last social media post, I can understand why they might think that."

Chewy rushed into Sam's room and jumped on the bed. The cat shot the dog a disdainful look, then jumped to the floor, stretched, and walked out of the room. Chewy bounded into Sam's lap and licked her face. Sam chuckled and pushed the dog off.

Dad stuck in his head. "You forgot to let Chewy back in, and Mom just called. She's turning into the subdivision. Time for dinner."

"Hang on," she told Makayla. "Hey, Dad?"

"Yeah?"

"It's still okay for Makayla to spend the night tomorrow, right, because her parents have that thing?"

"Of course. Mom's declared it pizza night, even though it's a Thursday."

Sam grinned. "You know, they haven't issued an AMBER Alert for Tam. Is that good or bad?"

He leaned against the door jam. "Well, it can go either way. Good is more people are alerted to his disappearance so if anyone knows where he is, they can call in, which would lead to him being found sooner. Bad is it sometimes puts people in a panic for nothing when the kid is just off sulking or pouting."

"I heard they took his cell phone to go through."

Before Dad could reply, Chewy started barking and raced from the room.

"Mom's home. Come on," Dad said before turning back down the hall.

"I'll call you after I eat," Sam told Makayla.

"Okay. Bye."

Sam rushed into the kitchen, ready to talk to Mom. As an investigative journalist, Mom sometimes thought of things in a different way. Maybe she'd have some suggestions or thoughts about Tam's disappearance.

She sure hoped so. By Sam's calculations, Tam had been missing for over eight hours, at least two of them right smack dab in the middle of a horrible storm. She whispered another prayer that he was okay, wherever he was.

CHAPTER FOUR

—So if any of you have seen Tam Lee or know of his whereabouts, please contact the Pulaski County Sheriff's Office immediately. Help us bring home one of our own Senators. ~Sam Sanderson reporting

Sam reread her article for the third time. It was good. Satisfied, she clicked the button to not only take the post live, but to send a copy to the Senator Speak faculty supervisor, Ms. Pape and also to Aubrey Damas. The editor would be ticked that Sam scooped her yet again, but Sam didn't care. This was about Tam and finding him. As the hours clicked by, Sam grew more and more worried.

Was he safe? Was he hungry? Scared? Alone? Dry?

Sam couldn't imagine being all alone somewhere, especially with the weather Little Rock had experienced today. Even if she'd gotten upset enough to run away, being alone wasn't exactly an ideal situation. Surely Tam was with someone he knew and trusted.

But what if he wasn't?

She stared at the list of newspaper staff members and their phone numbers sitting on her desk. Mom had asked if anyone had spoken to the friend Tam wanted to visit last night. Dad said he didn't know.

Luke Jensen. Sure, Sam tripped up around him because he was so incredibly cute, but this was reporting. This was about finding Tam. Sam couldn't let her personal feelings interfere with reporting, right? A good reporter could push aside her own emotions to get to the heart of a story . . . that's what Mom always said.

Sam let out a quick breath, then quickly dialed Luke's cell number before she could think of a gazillion good reasons not to have to talk to him.

"Hello." Even over the phone, Luke Jensen's voice held that high-wattage smile that made butterflies swarm in Sam's stomach.

"Hey, Luke. It's Sam. Sanderson. Sam Sanderson." She swallowed the groan. Could she sound any more like an idiot?

"I know. What's up?" He was kind enough not to make fun of her stammering.

"I guess you heard about Tam?"

"Yeah. A deputy came by to talk to me just a few minutes ago."

"Do you have any idea where he could be?" She held her breath as she'd been holding out a secret hope that Tam was just hiding out at Luke's.

"No. I'd asked him to come over last night because I was working on my EAST project and needed a little help. Tam said he'd be happy to help me, and asked if he could come stay over. We had planned it all, but in the end his dad said no because it was a school night."

Same thing Mrs. Lee had told the deputy. Sam chewed the inside of her bottom lip. "Was he really mad that his dad wouldn't let him go?"

"Like I told the cop, I wouldn't say he was all that mad. He seemed more annoyed that his dad didn't trust him. He complained that it wasn't like he ever got into trouble or anything, so he didn't understand why his dad was being so strict."

"Mmm." Maybe there was more to the family dynamics, like her dad had hinted.

"But he wasn't all angry and stuff. He said it more with a sigh than with anger. You know what I mean?"

Boy, did she. Mom could make Sam feel more like a dope when she used her disappointed tone than when she was mad. "Oh, yeah."

Luke laughed, but it sounded a little forced. "I guess we all know what that's like."

"So, you didn't talk to Tam after he told you he couldn't come over?"

"Well, after he posted on Facebook about his dad's

stupid rules, I sent him a private message and asked if he was okay. He said he was just blowing off steam and knew his dad would see it."

"So he posted it for his dad to see on purpose?" Wow, that really was brave for him to do that. Sam would be grounded for life.

"He said he hoped it would make his dad realize how ridiculous and outdated the rules were."

Maybe so, but Sam's dad would still ground her, and he'd make her delete the post. She might have even had to delete her Facebook page. "That's it?"

"Yeah. I just replied with *LOL*, and I didn't hear anything else from him."

Sam opened Facebook on her MacBook, then went to Tam's page. The post was still up. There were seventy-two likes on the post, but no comments.

"I'm worried about him, Sam," Luke said, his voice not as confident and strong as usual. "The cop acted like Tam ran away or something, but that's not like him."

"I know," Sam barely whispered. No matter about Dad's talk and the police's theory, she just couldn't wrap her mind around the idea that Tam would run away from home. "He doesn't even have his cell phone."

"Right. If Tam ran away, he would have certainly taken his cell phone. I told the cop that, but he shrugged it off. I hate that. Why do cops think we kids don't understand things? We're not stupid."

Even her dad sometimes acted like she couldn't understand certain things. "Oh, I hear you. But if he didn't run away, where could he be?" she asked.

"That's what worries me. His mom said she dropped him off at school this morning just before eight. I was there a little after eight and I never saw him."

"What do you think happened to him?" she asked, even as she continued to check out Tam's page on Facebook. A couple of his friends had already started posting comments on his wall like "Where are you?"

"I don't know. I told the cop I didn't have any idea, but the way he acted . . . I'm not sure he believed me," Luke said.

"I think they need to get the word out. The more people who know he's missing, the better chance of someone having seen him or something. I posted an article up on the school's blog. A few kids have already started posting on Tam's Facebook page, but they haven't issued an AMBER Alert on him yet."

"Wonder why that is?"

"I don't know. Dad says it's up to the deputy handling the case." That's what he'd told her over supper.

"Your dad can't work this case?" Luke asked.

"Not his jurisdiction, and the deputy didn't seem to want Dad's help." She took note of the time at the top of her computer task bar.

"Well, I think they need it. They need to do something."

"Yeah. The news is about to come on. I'm going to go watch and see if they mention Tam. Maybe they'll issue an AMBER Alert for him."

"I'll let you know if I hear anything, and you let me know if you find out anything, okay?"

"Sure. Thanks, Luke. Bye." Sam hung up and headed into the living room. She plopped on the couch across from the two recliners. Her dad sat in one of them.

"Where's Mom?" Sam asked.

"Doing laundry. You're watching the news?"

"I want to see if there's anything on about Tam."

Dad nodded, then turned up the volume as the music lead-in for the local news came on the air.

Sam found herself getting more and more frustrated as the news anchor jumped from news of a bank robbery to a fire in an abandoned lot to a promo for sports. Didn't anybody care that Tam was missing? Why weren't they putting out an AMBER Alert? Why weren't they organizing search parties?

The news faded into the first commercial break.

"Dad, why aren't they talking about Tam's disappearance?"

"There are several reasons why they wouldn't, pumpkin."

"Like what?" Sam knew she sounded a little snotty, but this was important.

"If it's believed Tam's a runaway."

"Everyone's already told the police that he didn't run away. Why won't they listen?"

"It's hard to explain. That Tam argued with his parents about not being allowed to go somewhere is a very common reason for junior high kids to take off. They usually show back up in a day or so, just long enough to save face, but not long enough to be really hungry."

"Tam's not like that, Dad. His mom told the cop that, I did, even Mrs. Trees told him Tam has never been in trouble and is a good kid. And if he was going to run away from home, he wouldn't have left his cell phone in his room."

"I'm not involved in the case, Sam, so I can't say for sure, but I'm pretty certain the sheriff's office has their reasons for treating the case more as a suspected runaway than anything else."

The news returned, going to a feature on a local businessman winning some award, then moved on to sports, which talked about the Razorback's track and baseball teams.

"Dad, what if they're wrong?"

"What?"

"What if the sheriff's office is wrong? What if they treat Tam like a runaway but he doesn't show back up in a day or so . . . what then?"

He ran a hand over the whisker stubble on his chin, scratching. "Then they'll have to look at things from a different angle."

"But they've wasted the day by not doing anything!"

"It's complicated, Sam."

"But that's what it will be, right? Wasting a day or so waiting for a runaway to come back, only when he doesn't, they have to scramble to figure out what really happened to him, right?"

"I'm sure they're working every angle they can. Police work isn't all cut and dried. A lot of time, it's gut instinct and looking at every detail a dozen different ways." Dad smiled. "I bet they're doing more than you think."

Sam shrugged. But what if they weren't? What if the police weren't doing a thing besides waiting for Tam to come home?

What if he was scared or hurt? What if he had been kidnapped and the Lees just hadn't received the ransom note yet?

Sam couldn't sit still. She headed to her room as soon as the news went into the final weather forecast. She didn't know what she could do, but knew she needed to do something. Anything.

Which, as far as she could tell, was more than the sheriff's office was doing.

CHAPTER FIVE

"Since you were so quick to write an article and get it posted yesterday, you can cover this morning's assembly on Tam's disappearance, *Samantha*." Aubrey's snooty voice carried across the cafeteria before school.

The smell of breakfast remnants filled the closed room, even though the serving line had just closed.

"Assembly?" Sam ignored Aubrey's snide tone and the use of her full name that Aubrey did just to annoy her.

"Yes. Mrs. Trees is having an assembly about Tam this morning. Ms. Pape sent me a text about it this morning." Aubrey smirked, gloating. She just loved knowing stuff before Sam did. "So I'm assigning you to cover it."

Sure enough, the school's custodial staff had started setting up the microphone on the cafeteria stage.

"Okay." Sam nodded at Aubrey, not caring that the editor thought it was a ho-hum assignment.

Aubrey turned and sauntered across the cafeteria toward her clique of friends.

Sam shook her head, disregarding her. "At least someone's going to talk about Tam disappearing without a trace," she said. The local news this morning hadn't announced the issuance of an AMBER Alert for him. Sam thought that very strange and even her dad said he'd thought there'd be some mention of his disappearance on the news, unless Tam had already returned home. With an assembly about his disappearance, that sliver of hope was gone.

Sam had asked her father about a Morgan Nick alert, which started in Arkansas back in 1995 when a girl named Morgan was abducted. Now it was an alert that went out over the broadcasting system. Dad had explained that Morgan Nick alerts were only issued when an abduction was confirmed or if the missing child had a mental or physical disability.

Bella Kelly, a fellow cheerleader, sat across from Sam and Makayla. "Yeah, my dad's coming this morning to report on the assembly and Tam's disappearance." Bella's dad was a prominent newscaster for the local FOX affiliate.

Sam nodded, grateful at least there would finally be something on the news about Tam. She had checked Tam's Facebook page this morning and there was no new post from him. She'd overheard her Dad saying on the phone this morning that the Lees hadn't heard from Tam yet. Sam could imagine how worried her own parents would be if she were missing.

Then again, if she were missing, Dad would have the entire Little Rock Police Department out searching for her. The church would get involved . . . hey, that was a thought: what church did the Lees belong to? Maybe they could start a search or something.

"Do you know what church Tam goes to?" Sam asked Makayla.

"No, why?"

Sam shrugged. "I just wondered if maybe his church was organizing a search or something for him." The longer he was missing with nothing being done, the angrier Sam got. "It's about time someone started doing something, you know?"

Makayla nodded as the first bell rang. The noise level almost exploded as kids stood and shuffled and talked louder.

Mrs. Trees popped the microphone with her index finger, filling the cafeteria with three quick *boops* over the speakers. Everyone stopped moving and talking. "Students, if you would, please hurry along to your homeroom class. Instead of activity period this morning, you'll be coming back to the cafeteria for an assembly. Thank you."

The racket erupted again as everyone rushed to spill out of the cafeteria.

"You coming?" Makayla asked, lifting her backpack to her shoulder.

"No, I think I'm going to try and talk with Mrs. Trees. Get what info I can."

"Good luck with that. I've got to put my bag for your house in my locker, so I'll see you in the assembly."

Sam set her backpack against the wall, then made her way toward the stage, weaving around all the sixth, seventh, and eighth graders trying to squeeze out of the double doors. "Mrs. Trees . . . Mrs. Trees," she called out as she got closer to the principal.

"Yes, Sam?" Mrs. Trees turned from the deputy standing just off stage.

"I'm covering the assembly for the *Senator Speak*. Is there any information you can give me before it starts?" Sam pulled out a notebook and pen. Although cell phones weren't banned from school, technically, since the bell had rung, she wasn't supposed to use one. Sam wasn't about to do anything to get in trouble right now.

The principal took a moment's hesitation, glanced at the deputy, then back to Sam. "Deputy Jameson will be making an announcement regarding Tam's disappearance and asking if anyone has any information regarding the situation."

"Is there any new information?" Sam glanced to the deputy to include him.

Mrs. Trees turned to Deputy Jameson, who stepped closer. "We're going to be asking if anyone has any information regarding Tam, to let us know."

"We've set it up so they can write what they know on the index cards being handed out at the door and drop them in a box on the way out so no one will know who responded," Mrs. Trees said.

That was actually a really good idea. "Can I help?"

Mrs. Trees smiled. "Sure. You can help Mrs. Creegle hand out the index cards."

That wasn't exactly what Sam meant, but she nodded. Thoughts of Tam being alone and scared or hurt kept bouncing around inside her head.

As if she knew she'd just been mentioned, the guidance counselor joined the small group on the stage. "I have the box ready. Do you want it by the door now, or wait until near the end of the assembly?" Mrs. Creegle asked the principal.

Mrs. Trees glanced at the deputy. "Why don't we wait until the end of the assembly? That way, no one will bother it until we collect any index cards."

"Sam here is going to assist you in handing out the cards," Mrs. Trees told the counselor.

Mrs. Creegle smiled. "Thank you, Sam. Come on, the bell's about to ring and the teachers will be bringing their classes in."

Sam followed her to the main double doors.

"You stand on the outside here and hand a card to each person who enters, and I'll hand them out for those that enter by the media center." Mrs. Creegle handed Sam a stack of white index cards with faint blue writing lines, then turned and headed to the other side of the cafeteria.

"Hello, Sam," a man said.

Sam glanced up, recognizing Bella's dad standing beside a man holding a video camera. "Hi, Mr. Kelly."

The cameraman sat up close to the wall, but with a clear view of the podium on the stage. Mr. Kelly moved toward the stage and spoke to the principal.

The bell rang, and noise filled the room once more as teachers and students headed to the assembly. Sam shoved cards in kids' hands as fast as she could.

"Students, please quickly take a seat. You'll need to squeeze together since we're only having one assembly. It'll be a little cramped, but I promise we'll keep it short," Mrs. Trees said over the microphone.

Breathing became harder for Sam as the cafeteria was soon packed to capacity. So many people taking up space and sucking up air. There wasn't a spare seat on the benches. Sam stepped out over the doors' threshold and inhaled deeply. At least the air from the breezeway was cool.

"Students, we have special guests here this morning who want to speak to you," Mrs. Trees said into the microphone from the stage. "I expect each of you to be respectful and pay careful attention."

Everyone grew quieter as two uniformed deputies walked onto the stage.

"Hello. I'm Deputy Jameson with the Pulaski County

Sheriff's Office. This is my partner, Deputy Malone." His voice boomed over the cafeteria, commanding attention.

Sam stepped back into the room and leaned against the yellow-painted, cinderblock wall.

"I'm sure most of you now know that Tam Lee is missing."

Sam nodded. Exactly: missing. Why weren't they pulling out all the stops to find him? Organizing search parties? Putting out an AMBER Alert?

"The last time anyone saw him was here, yesterday morning before school. He did not just disappear without someone knowing something about it. We believe someone saw him leave. We believe someone here knows where Tam is."

What? Sam pushed off the wall and grabbed a pen, making notes on an index card for her article.

"We're asking for your help. Someone here saw what happened."

Really? What did they know? Sam chewed the end cap of the ballpoint pen.

"You were given a card when you came into the room. We're asking everyone to privately write on their card. If you saw Tam, know what happened, or have any information, we ask that you write it down. If you know nothing, just write the word "nothing" on your card. This way, no one will know if you tell anything, and it's totally anonymous since everyone will turn in a card to . . ."

Mrs. Creegle rushed across the room and held up a

big box with a slot cut out. It was the box the school used for their student council voting and homecoming court voting.

"Everyone will drop their card in this box on their way out of the assembly." Deputy Jameson motioned toward Mrs. Creegle and her box.

"You don't have to give your name," Deputy Malone said, stepping up to the microphone. His voice wasn't as deep and commanding as his partner's. "But we know everyone wants to help their fellow student if they can."

Students began to whisper. Sam shoved her notes into the back pocket of her jeans.

"Students, please write on your card as the deputies instructed, then we'll file out, in an organized manner, so everyone can drop their card into the box," Mrs. Trees announced.

Rustling. Voices. Bangs on the tables. Sam ignored the noise and Mrs. Creegle and moved to the stage stairs. The principal and deputies were talking on the stage. Sam turned to get a better angle to listen as the first sixth grade teacher stood and led his students toward the doors.

"You can use the table in the conference room to review all the cards," Mrs. Trees told the deputies.

Sam swallowed her squeal of excitement. They were going to sort through the cards here! She moved to hold the box with Mrs. Creegle. Maybe if she was helping, they wouldn't make a big deal out of her being in the office. Surely she could figure out some way to stay in the office while they went through the cards.

"Thanks, Sam," the counselor told her in between students dropping the cards in the box.

Sam took on more of the weight, almost bearing all of it. "I've got it, Mrs. Creegle."

"Are you certain?"

The box grew heavier by the minute with the number of cards going in, but Sam could do this. She would. "Sure. I can bring it to the office when everyone's out."

"Thanks." Mrs. Creegle headed through the doors herself.

Sam's internal grin almost snuck across her face. She had her *in*! Mom was always telling her a good journalist looked for ways into the story, not just the outside reporting, but getting *in*to the story. This was hers.

The last row of students followed their teacher toward the doors. Sam's elation nearly plummeted as Aubrey Damas approached, smirk planted firmly on her snooty face. Nikki Cole, who was actually a nice person but seemed to be content with spouting regurgitated Aubrey venom, followed at her heels.

"Nice doorman duty, *Samantha*." Aubrey pushed her card through the slot.

Sam let the box go for only a split second, but it made Aubrey jump back, right into Nikki, thinking that it was going to fall and hit her. Sam snickered.

Aubrey narrowed her eyes. "You're so evil, *Samantha*. Just evil."

Struggling not to laugh, Sam averted her eyes. Her gaze locked with Luke Jensen's. "Hey," he said as he shoved his card quickly into the box.

"H-Hi." Well, at least she got a whole word out this time.

He hesitated, as though he wanted to say something else, but then flashed her a killer smile and moved on.

"Hey, do-gooder." Felicia Adams, Sam's newest friend, was the last student in line. In eighth grade, Felicia recently transferred to Robinson after being expelled from a private school. Everyone had thought she was bad news with an even worse attitude—Sam knew differently.

Felicia, who had been a cheerleader and on the newspaper and yearbook staff at the private school she'd attended before Robinson, had been forced by her mother to sit out of all extra-curricular activities at Robinson as a form of punishment. Soon enough, her parents and the school had allowed Felicia to join the newspaper staff, and she'd been there ever since.

She still had a rough attitude, but Sam appreciated her standing up for what she believed in. "Hi, troublemaker."

Felicia grinned. "Have you heard anything new?" Her grin disappeared. "Anything about Tam?"

Sam shook her head as she shifted the box to her hip

to hold it more easily. "I've not heard anything new, but the police seem to think that somebody here knows something."

Nodding, Felicia grabbed the other side of the box. "The way they're acting, yeah, it sure seems like that."

Together the girls carried the box to the office. Sam used her hip to hold her side as she struggled with the office door. Mr. Kelly quickly shot off the bench to help them.

"Take that right to the conference room, Sam," Mrs. Darrington said even while she narrowed her eyes at Felicia. Obviously, she was one of the people who still didn't appreciate Felicia's in-your-face attitude.

"I'll catch you later, do-gooder." Felicia waited until Sam had control of the whole box before she let go and left the office.

"Thanks." Sam trudged down the hall, around the corner, but stopped just short of the conference room as she heard Mrs. Trees speaking.

"Here's the note the security guard found in Tam's locker," she said.

Sam froze, her heart pounding so hard she was sure the principal would hear it echoing in her ribcage. Note?

"I wish you would have waited for our team to open his locker," Deputy Malone's softer, but right now scarier, voice carried into the hall. "Evidence might have been contaminated."

Evidence? Sam gripped the box tighter.

"I'm sorry. We didn't expect to find anything . . . we wanted to be diligent in finding out what happened to our student." Mrs. Trees sounded quite indignant.

"We'll have a team go through the locker this afternoon, after school. No sense in alerting the other students to what's going on," the deputy said.

Sam chewed the inside of her lip and bent her head. What *was* going on?

"Any idea who this *J.T.* is? And *what* was set for the morning? Any idea what morning the note references?"

Sam inhaled . . . her nose tingled . . .

Ah-choo!

CHAPTER SIX

Busted!

Sam rushed into the conference room, plopped the box on the table, then sneezed again, but not before she noticed a piece of notebook paper with fold creases all over it.

"Are you okay, Sam?" Mrs. Trees asked.

She sniffed and nodded. "Just allergies."

"It is that time of year. Thank you for bringing the box." The principal stared at her. "Mrs. Darrington will give you a pass to go back to class."

"Actually, Mrs. Trees . . ." Sam scrambled to think of an excuse, any excuse, to stay. "I'm more than happy to help sort the cards."

"That won't be necessary," Deputy Jameson said as he popped the top open and began pulling out stacks of cards. Deputy Malone did the same.

Sam moved closer to Mrs. Trees, so she could just make out some of the writing on the notebook paper. "Well, I do have a few more questions for you. For the paper's article."

The intercom in the conference room squalled. "Mrs. Trees?" Mrs. Darrington's voice came over the little speaker. "Mr. Kelly from FOX is waiting to speak with you."

"Send him to my office." Mrs. Trees shook her head at Sam. "Obviously, now is not a good time to talk, Sam."

"Yes, ma'am." Sam took a second to try one more time to read the note on the table as the principal crossed the hall to her office.

The note, written in pencil, read:

All set for in the morning.

—J.T.

The deputy cleared his throat and shot her a disapproving stare, then reached over and grabbed the note.

"Well, I guess I'll go back to class," Sam said, stepping into the hall just as Bella's dad turned the corner into Mrs. Trees' office.

"How are you, Mr. Kelly?"

His reply was cut off by the office door closing.

Sam stepped out of the conference room's doorway, but didn't rush toward the front office. She did a mental rundown of all the eighth graders she knew. Who was J.T.? No one came to mind with that nickname or with those initials. She needed to get to the library and look at last year's yearbook.

"Sam, do you need a pass back to class?" Mrs. Darrington stood in the hallway, staring at her.

Sam had been so lost in thought she hadn't even heard the secretary approach. "Yes, ma'am." She followed Mrs. Darrington to the front office.

The secretary typed on her computer, then a yellow pass printed out of the little badge printer on the front counter. "Thanks," Sam said as she tore it off, and an idea hit her.

Maybe she didn't need to go manually look through the yearbook in the library, which wouldn't even have new students for this year or transfers in it anyway. What she needed was to get into the system's badge database. Every single student had to have a student badge that had to be worn at all times.

Sam smiled as she stepped out of the office. Makayla!

"You want me to what?" Makayla raised her eyebrows.

Sam smiled as cheese-ily as she could. "I need you to get into the student database and find out who has the nickname J.T. or those initials."

"Sam, you know I love you and usually will do

anything to help you, but this time? This time, you're asking too much." Makayla stuck a Cheeto into her mouth and crunched for emphasis. "Hacking into the student database would get me immediately expelled."

"It's really important. I wouldn't ask if it wasn't."

Makayla swallowed then took a sip from her bottle of water. "Yes, you would. You have before."

"And when it's been important, you've helped." Sam snatched a chip from Makayla's plastic bag. "Just like this time."

Makayla grabbed the Cheeto back before Sam could take a bite. "This is beyond anything else I've done to help you." She leaned closer to Sam. "You're good with computers too. Why don't you look it up?"

"Oh, I might be good, but you're a computer ninja and you know it. You can do in ten minutes what it'd take me hours to do."

Makayla shook her head. "Don't try to flatter me. You aren't going to butter me up to get me in big trouble."

"But you could do it so easily when you're working in Mrs. Creegle's office."

"No."

Felicia squeezed onto the bench next to Sam. "What's going on, do-gooder?"

"Causing trouble, or trying to," Makayla mumbled.

Great. If Mac was dead set on not getting into the

computer system, Sam had to figure out another way. She faced Felicia. "Hey, do you know anybody called J.T.?"

"No, should I?"

Sam quickly told her about the note the police had found.

"If y'all don't know who J.T. is, I sure don't." Felicia grabbed one of Makayla's Cheetos. "I bet the police think Tam probably went to meet this J.T. yesterday morning, and that's why they're acting like he ran away."

"Even if he did meet whoever J.T. is, Tam's still missing now. He's been gone over twenty-four hours." Sam reached for Makayla's cookie.

Mac slapped her hand. "But at least the police are doing something now, right? I saw Bella's dad here. Does this mean they're finally issuing an AMBER Alert?"

"I don't know. They didn't announce it and they certainly didn't tell me. I couldn't even hang around to see if they got a lead from the index cards." Sam took a sip of her water. "I don't think Deputy Jameson likes me very much."

Felicia snorted. "No cop likes me." She nudged Sam. "No offense to your dad."

"Speaking of your dad, maybe you could ask him to see if he can find out anything," Makayla suggested.

"Seriously?" Sam put the cap back on her empty water bottle. "You know how Dad is, Mac. I swear, I think he'd go out of his way not to help me."

"Well, you have kind of disobeyed him a time or

two for the sake of a story," Makayla said with a sheepish grin.

"But this time, it's not about a story." Although, if she helped crack the case she could write an article before it hit the local news, and she'd really secure her nomination for editor next year. "At least, not primarily. I'm more worried about Tam than a story."

"Yeah, me too. He's always gone out of his way to be nice to me, and I can't say that about many people here," Felicia said.

"I don't know him, except through you," Makayla told Sam, "but it's scary to think that a kid can just disappear from our campus without anyone noticing."

Lana rushed to their little group and squeezed in on the other side of Makayla. "Guess what?" She didn't give anyone a chance to say anything before she started talking. "I had a dentist appointment this morning, so Mom just checked me in. We were in the office waiting for the dentist to fax my excuse because Mom forgot to get one while we were there. I mean, the lady was talking to Mom about the changes in our insurance plan, and Mom's pretty upset that our deductible went up again—"

"Lana!" Sam really liked her friend, but sometimes Lana got off on a side street during a conversation. This was just a prime example.

"Sorry. Anyway, while we were waiting, I overheard Mrs. Trees talking to Mrs. Darrington in the little office right next to the sick room."

Sam nodded, knowing the space well. She had stood there to eavesdrop herself a time or two.

"So Mrs. Trees tells Mrs. Darrington that the police got a lead from two students. The same lead from both of them, so the police are pretty positive it's legitimate."

So that must mean two index cards had the same info.

"Mrs. Trees told Mrs. Darrington to call Darby French's parent or guardian and tell them the deputies need to question their daughter." Lana grabbed the last one of Makayla's fruit snacks and popped it into her mouth. "Mrs. Trees told Mrs. Darrington to tell them to please come to the school immediately."

Darby French . . . Darby French. Name didn't ring a bell with Sam.

"And then the fax came through, so I had to give it to Mrs. Darrington and then she printed me my pass, so I don't know anything more."

"Who is Darby French?" Sam asked.

Lana and Felicia both shook their heads.

"I don't know, either," Makayla said.

"Well, her initials are certainly not J.T.," Sam said.

The bell rang and they all got up from the table. Sam linked her arm through Makayla's. "You know, you could look for information on Darby French while you're searching for the mysterious J.T. when you're doing counselor's aide today."

Makayla grunted. "Nope, you aren't tricking me into

really getting into trouble by getting into the system for not one, but two searches."

"Aw, c'mon, Mac." Sam tossed her trash into the can. She could whine all she wanted, but she recognized that look on her best friend's face—she wasn't going to do any searches. Sam was going to have to figure it out on her own.

"No. And why does everybody always eat *my* lunch?"

CHAPTER SEVEN

Sam chewed the inside of her bottom lip as she sat down at one of the class computer stations. Since Makayla wouldn't tap into the guidance counselor's computer, Sam had to figure out who Darby and J.T. were. Since she had little chance of hacking into the student database, and she wasn't going to chance getting busted by trying and failing, she figured her best option at this point was to learn as much about Tam as she could.

While she didn't have a lot of ideas on how to go about that, she did have one, and she just so happened to be her own best resource on that avenue. As one of the returning EAST students who had participated in various training workshops at the EAST conference last year, and as a trainer for the new EAST facilitators in the district over the summer, Sam was one of the administrators in the system. She had full access to go into every student's project and view the files. Sometimes, Mrs. Shine even asked her to check some of the other classes' project progress.

Tam had EAST for sixth period. Maybe for his project, he had a partner who would turn out to know who the mysterious J.T. or Darby was. Sam could definitely check and see if there was any connection to anyone like that.

She glanced up over the computer monitor to Mrs. Shine's desk—the teacher had her nose buried in her laptop. Not that the teacher would fault Sam for looking. Besides, Sam was Mrs. Shine's favorite student, you could ask anyone. But still. Sam felt a little like a snoop, but if she could find out something that could lead her to her missing friend . . . she swallowed, opened the network, then connected to the EASTSERVER. She scrolled through the list of student users until she found Tam's name.

After checking to make sure Mrs. Shine was still engrossed at her desk, Sam opened Tam's files. She clicked on the one titled "Pictures" only to find it empty. Same with "Research" and "Overview." Every single file under Tam's project was blank. Even his reports file was empty. There was no way Mrs. Shine would allow anybody to go this far along in the semester without turning in at least a couple of project reports.

Sam closed the program and restarted it, then accessed Tam's files again. Empty. It made no sense. What had happened to all his documents? Pictures? Research?

She maneuvered into Mrs. Shine's documents. The teacher might be less understanding if she caught Sam going through her files. Sam glanced at her desk. One of the eighth graders had a book laid out in front of Mrs. Shine and pointed, the two in deep conversation. No time like the present.

Sam scrolled through the teacher's documents. She'd sorted by class period. Sam opened the sixth period folder, then scrolled down to Tam's name and clicked on that folder. There was only one document inside and it was titled: Project Details. Sam opened the pdf and began reading the brief overview.

> Awareness of possible danger is critical to the safety of children. Awareness of physical surroundings, potentially suspect people, and Internet safety measures should all be integral teachings to children who use the Internet. The Arkansas board of education requires students to take a variety of standardized tests, yet for something as critical as child safety and online child safety, there are no requirements. This project will prove the need for mandatory safety education for all students of upper elementary schools. Recommended in-class workshops such as the NetSmartz® and KidSmartz workshops, offered by the National Center for Missing and Exploited

> Children. These workshops serve as educational programs, teaching children about online safety as well as educating families about abduction prevention and child empowerment to practice safer behaviors. These programs offer free, age-appropriate resources including videos, games, presentations, and classroom lessons to help children learn how to protect themselves and their friends online.

Sam caught her bottom lip between her teeth as she read bullet points of facts that were apparently part of the presentation of his research.

- Approximately eight hundred thousand children under the age of eighteen were reported missing. Of that, more than two hundred thousand were abducted by family members.
- Ninety-three percent of teens ages twelve to seventeen use the Internet. Eighty percent use it over three times a week.
- The first three hours are the most critical when trying to locate a missing child.
- The National Center for Missing and Exploited Children has assisted law enforcement in the recovery of more than 205,550 missing children since it was founded in 1984.
- Their recovery rate for missing children is currently ninety-seven percent.

"Sam, could you come help Joy with the Blender software, please?" Mrs. Shine jerked Sam's focus away from the computer screen.

"Uh, y-yes, ma'am." Sam quickly closed all the folders and files, backed out of everything, then stood and headed to the teacher's desk.

"I'm having a hard time getting the graphic to actually move," Joy, the eighth grader, told Sam as she led her to the computer she'd been working on.

Sam helped Joy figure out the animation problem easily enough and wanted to go back into Mrs. Shine's file and read the rest about Tam's project. She hadn't even found out if he had a partner. Epic failure.

"Hey, Sam?"

She looked up and smiled at Marcus Robertson. He was in eighth grade and the school paper's photographer. He stood in front of her desk and motioned to the chair beside her. "Mind if I sit and talk with you for a minute?"

"Of course not." He'd always been really nice to Sam, but he didn't exactly seek her out like this very often.

He sat down, then pushed the chair back a little bit. "Have you heard anything new about Tam?"

She had, but it was all unofficial at this point, and she was pretty sure she'd get in hot water if she told everybody about the note before the deputy could do anything with it. "They haven't said anything that you've heard, have they?" Sam despised someone answering her question with a question, but sometimes . . . well, sometimes it was just the best way to reply. "I'm really worried about him."

"Me, too. I saw you taking up the index cards. Do you know what they're specifically looking for?"

Every warning bell echoed in Sam's head. "How do you know they were looking for something specific?" Even she didn't know that.

"Uh. Well. The way they were . . . uh . . . asking. And . . . uh, talking." Marcus blushed a little.

"You should probably tell me what you're trying to hide, because you aren't doing such a great job."

His cheeks turned pinker. "Look, it's probably nothing . . ."

What was it with people? "Marcus!" she hissed, fighting against screaming out loud at him. Frustration swiped at her chest like BabyKitty sharpening her claws.

"Okay, okay. It's just that Tam was supposed to meet a friend of ours yesterday morning but she was late meeting him, so now . . . well, she's worried that maybe he went to look for her and something happened to him."

Sam was pretty sure her heart just skipped a beat. "Where was he supposed to meet her?"

Marcus looked at his feet. "Around the side of the school."

"For what?"

He snagged her gaze and slowly gave a single shoulder shrug. "He's been helping her with pre-AP Algebra. Like tutoring."

Yeah, Sam could so see Tam helping someone with math—he was good at it and he was sweet enough to help anyone who asked. But . . . "Around the side of the building? Before school?" *That* she couldn't quite see Tam doing. As his mom had told the deputy, Tam was too much of a rule follower.

Marcus shook his head. "From what she told me, they usually studied together during activity period in the library."

That made sense. "Why were they meeting in a different place and time than usual?"

"I don't know."

"Did you ask her?" Sam curled her hands into tight balls. How could people expect to learn something and not ask any questions? That drove her up the wall.

He shook his head again. "She's really freaked out about him being missing."

Duh! "Aren't we all?" Sam swallowed back the sarcasm.

"Yeah, but she's scared because they told her the police want to talk to her and have called her mom to come up. She's terrified they're going to haul her downtown or something. I told her that was crazy." He gave Sam a weak smile. "That is crazy, isn't it? I mean, I know your dad's a cop and all, so I thought maybe you might have an idea what the protocol is."

"Your friend is Darby French?"

Marcus nodded. "How'd you know?"

Again, time to answer a question with a question. "How do you know Darby?"

"We have history together." He leaned forward and lowered his voice. "You don't think they'll make her go to the police station or something, do you? I mean, they wouldn't do that to kids, right?"

"I don't know. This is the sheriff's case, not the city police like where my dad works." Sam let out a long breath. "I posted the article yesterday afternoon about Tam missing. Didn't Darby see that? Or didn't she wonder when he wasn't at school? Why didn't she come forward?" Sam didn't know the girl, but her story sounded a little fishy.

"I asked her why she didn't tell anyone she was supposed to meet Tam in the morning, especially when everyone said he'd gone missing before school."

"What'd she say?" Sam pinched her lips together and breathed slowly through her nose.

"She said that she couldn't tell anybody why she was late. When she got here, the tardy bell had already rung. She had to get an unexcused pass, and worried Tam would be upset with her for not making their meeting. But when she got to their math class and he wasn't there, she figured he was sick or had a doctor's appointment or something since he was rarely absent."

Very true. Sam couldn't recall one day he'd missed this year.

"Darby said she didn't know anything was wrong

until she read your article online yesterday afternoon. She freaked because she thinks maybe Tam got worried when she didn't show and went looking for her or something and then something happened to him." Marcus glanced over his shoulder toward Mrs. Shine for a minute, then back at Sam. "That's silly, right?"

Sam didn't know, but she could see that Tam could have gone looking for her. If he thought she'd be there and she didn't show, he would have gotten worried. Yeah, Tam was like that. "Where would he have gone to look for her? Wouldn't the logical place be the cafeteria, to see if she forgot or something?" That's what she would do.

"I don't know. It doesn't make any sense." Marcus shook his head. "But now she's freaking out."

"I don't know why she didn't say anything to anybody last night when she found out he was missing. That's important information." Could be important to the case. "I'm not sure, but I think that's like tampering with a police investigation or something." She was pretty sure she'd heard her father say something like that before.

Marcus's eyes widened. "That's what she's really freaking out about, but she says she can't tell anybody why she was so late for school. She told me that she was sworn to secrecy."

"What does that mean?" Sam didn't like this, not one bit. It sounded like Darby knew something more. What kind of person was she?

"I don't know. She said her parents were going to be furious."

"Students, save your work and log off the computers. The bell's about to ring," Mrs. Shine announced.

"Look, if you see Darby later today, try to get her to tell you why she was late." Sam shut down the computer.

"I doubt I'll see her. She was called out of class to the office last period. I'm sure because her parents were here."

Sam frowned. "Well, I saw that the deputy's car was gone before I came into EAST, so if the police are going to question her, they're doing it somewhere besides school." How disappointing. How was she supposed to figure out what was going on?

"Man, just what she was scared of." He stood and pushed his chair under the table. "It's gonna be okay, right?"

"I don't know, Marcus." She had to figure out a way to find out what Darby told the police. "If she doesn't come back to school, maybe you should call her and see how it went." She didn't add—*And get the information about why they were meeting and why she was late and why she couldn't tell anyone* but she thought it.

"Yeah, I guess I'll have to do that."

The bell rang. Sam squeezed Marcus's upper arm. "It'll all work out, Marcus."

"I hope so."

"See you in last period," Sam said as she grabbed her folder and smiled at Mrs. Shine before heading to her locker.

"Hey, Sam," Grace Brannon greeted her in the breezeway of the seventh grade ramp.

"Hi, Grace."

"What's the latest on Tam?"

Sam supposed everyone assumed she knew all the latest information because she posted the news articles on the school's blog, which reminded her that she needed to update the site during seventh period with notes regarding the assembly. "They haven't said anything new that I know of." Sam quickly switched out her folders and notebooks.

"It's sad. I checked Tam's Twitter account this morning and it's so strange not to see a recent post from him. He usually makes some type of *have a great day* comment every morning on his accounts."

"Yeah, I know." But Sam's mind was going in a different direction. Maybe, just maybe, Tam was friends with J.T. on Facebook or Twitter. Since Makyala wasn't interested in searching the student database for somebody, this could be a way for her to look. Even if it was creeping.

"I heard they're pretty sure he ran away from home." Grace shut her locker and faced Sam. "I wouldn't ever suspect him of that, but I guess it's true that you really don't know people."

Sam shut her locker as well. "I don't believe he ran away. That's just not Tam. He's too . . . too . . . responsible to run away. Everything he does serves a good purpose. I just can't accept him running away because his dad told him no."

"Then why are the police treating it like that?"

"I don't really know. Dad says there are usually things the police know that aren't public knowledge." Oh, how many times had he told Sam that?

"I suppose." Grace started to take a step away, then turned back to Sam. "Are you praying for him?"

That stopped Sam cold. Grace had mentioned before that her family wasn't Christian, but Sam hadn't stopped mentioning church or inviting Grace to some of her youth group events. They'd had a couple of conversations regarding faith and God. "Yes. Yes, I am praying for him. That he's safe and will be home soon."

"You aren't asking God why Tam's missing?"

Sam shook her head. "No. Why he's missing isn't as important right now as him being safe and coming home soon."

Grace nodded, then turned away and disappeared into the throng of other kids.

She should probably go after her and explain a little more, but the bell rang, and Sam ran inside her class, whispering a prayer for God to show her ways to share her faith.

CHAPTER EIGHT

Sam popped her knuckles and leaned back against her headboard. She tugged the laptop on top of her throw pillow on her lap. "I still can't believe you refused to help me."

"I didn't refuse to help," Makayla replied from the desk in Sam's room. "I refused to hack into the school's database for you, which is a smart move."

"You wouldn't have had to hack. You're a counselor's aide, so you have access to Mrs. Creegle's computer."

"Sam! That's wrong."

Grinning, Sam shook her head. "Okay, okay. But since you wouldn't look for me, I have to stalk Tam's social media pages. It's all your fault I'm becoming a creeper."

"Like you aren't creepy enough already." Mac laughed, causing BabyKitty to open her eyes and stare at her. The cat's tail twitched in disapproval of her nap being disturbed.

"Don't tell your mom I'm a creeper, or she'll never let you sleep over again." Sam opened her Facebook page and typed Tam's name in the search box.

"I think she secretly hopes your dad being a cop will make me, I don't know, want to be a lawyer."

Sam broke her focus from Tam's profile picture to look at her bestie. "She's still riding that bus? Wanting you to be a lawyer?"

"Sadly, yes." Makayla shook her head. "I don't know why, either. I've never been combative, argumentative, or wanted to debate."

"Well, I don't know about not being argumentative," Sam teased.

Makayla narrowed her eyes and made duck lips.

Sam laughed. "Have you told your mom that you don't want to be a lawyer?"

"Not exactly." Makayla stopped smiling and shook her head.

"What does that mean? You either have or you haven't."

"It's not that simple." Makayla twisted in the desk's chair and tucked her feet under her. "I've hinted that it takes so much time and money to become a lawyer, and most of them starting out these days just don't make the income they once did."

"What does she say to that?"

"She just says that such things are worth it in the long run."

Sam leaned the back of her head against the pillow. "Why don't you just flat out tell her you don't want to become a lawyer?"

"Because then she'll ask me what I do want to be, and I just don't know." Makayla shifted, tucking her feet under the other side of the chair.

"We're not even thirteen. We don't have to know what we want to be when we grow up," Sam said.

"You do. You've always known."

So true. "But that's because I grew up hearing Mom's stories and seeing her articles. She let me sit in her lap as she wrote when I was a toddler. Of course I want to be a journalist. I was raised with an excitement for trying to uncover the truth, for exposing what needed to be. It's a part of who I am."

"You're lucky. You're so sure of yourself and what you want to do." Makayla used that wistful voice she sometimes used when she talked about a break in a computer code creation or something along that path that went way over Sam's head. "It's helpful to know so you can make a plan. You have one, right?"

"I do, but I'm a freak, you know that." Sam stuck out her tongue. "And you love me anyway."

"Yeah, yeah, yeah. You're lucky I do, or you'd be in big trouble." Makayla's smile returned.

"Okay, time to become super creeper." Sam popped her knuckles again.

"Stop doing that. It's gross."

"You're just jealous you can't crack your knuckles." Sam laughed as she clicked on the link for Tam's friends, then started scrolling for anybody whose name started with a J.

"I wouldn't want to. Haven't you heard it'll make your knuckles bigger and give you arthritis when you're older?"

Sam stopped scrolling through Tam's Facebook friends. "You're kidding, right? That's an old myth."

Makayla shook her head. "My mother says that's why my grandmother has such horrible arthritis."

"Well, my dad used to stay on mine and Mom's case about cracking our knuckles, so Mom finally had enough and interviewed a leading rheumatologist. He assured her that cracking or popping our knuckles would not cause arthritis, nor would it make our knuckles bigger."

"I'm so telling my mother."

"But, he did tell Mom that in over fifty percent of those who cracked their knuckles, when they were older they had issues with their hands swelling."

"Hmm. And yet, you still pop yours?"

Sam grinned. "Yeah, yeah. I know." She turned back to the computer.

"The only friends I'm seeing of Tam's whose names

start with a J are: Jared Hopkins, who's on newspaper with us, Jefferson Cole, Nikki's little brother, a James Seymour, a Jane Rogers, and . . ." Sam bounced on the bed. "One Jason Turner."

BabyKitty jumped off the bed and ran from the room. Chewy gave chase down the hall.

"Who's Jason Turner?" Makayla asked, turning from her computer.

"I don't know, but let's see what I can find out." Sam clicked on Jason's name and brought up his Facebook page, then clicked on the About button. She read aloud, "Attends Joe T. Robinson High School. Loves computers, anime, and golf."

"High school? What grade is he in?"

Sam scrolled. "Hang on. Oh, he's a junior. Eleventh." She looked at Makayla. "I wouldn't have picked Tam as a person to have a lot of high school friends, would you?"

Makayla shook her head while Sam creeped a little more.

"He's in EAST." Sam wrinkled her nose. "I don't remember meeting him with the high school team at conference last year."

"Oh, you know everybody in EAST now, even the high school program?" Makayla teased.

Sam shrugged. "I just met a lot of the teams last year at conference." As one of the administrators, she helped keep Mrs. Shine's notes about the conference organized, and that included the correspondence with the high school and other facilitators. Thinking about Mrs. Shine's notes reminded Sam of what she'd found out in EAST today. "Hey, guess what?"

Makayla spun the desk chair around so she could prop her feet on the side of Sam's bed. "What?"

"Since you weren't willing to help me investigate—"

"You mean go into the student database without permission and get expelled."

"Whatever." Sam grinned. "Anyway, I pulled up Tam's EAST project in the computer today."

Makayla frowned. "Are you supposed to do that?"

"Mrs. Shine has asked me to look at stuff for her before, so it's fine."

Makayla raised one eyebrow.

"She has." Sam tossed a throw pillow at Makayla's head. "Anyway, all the files in his project are blank. Everything. Not even his project reports are in there, and I know Mrs. Shine has graded us on at least two this semester."

"Mrs. Shine wouldn't have allowed him an extension or something?"

Sam shook her head. "Not like this, not with conference coming up next month. We're up for a Founder's Award. No way would she let it slide." The Founder's Award was the highest award in EAST. It went to the school that best demonstrated the overall purpose and mission of EAST and it was quite the honor to even be named a finalist in the running. This was the first year the school was a finalist.

"Then what do you think is going on?"

"Well, I checked Mrs. Shine's files of the class's projects and I just found his project overview notes about making some workshops on Internet and child safety mandatory." She crossed her legs under the laptop on her bed.

Makayla wiped cat hair from her jeans. "Isn't that a co-winky-dink that Tam's project is about children's safety and now he's missing?"

"I know." Sam glanced back to Jason Turner's Facebook page. "You know, I've been thinking Tam was taken or something, even though Dad says the sheriff's office must be pretty sure he wasn't abducted if they haven't issued an AMBER Alert or anything."

Makayla moved from the chair to lay across the foot of Sam's bed and prop up on a pillow to stare at Sam. "Yeah, go on."

"But what if that didn't happen? What if Tam went somewhere?"

"What do you mean?"

Sam set the MacBook on the bed and stood up. She thought better when she paced. "The note said: *All set for in the morning* and was signed by *J.T.*, right?"

Makayla sat up and nodded. "That's what you said."

"What if this Jason Turner is the J.T. in the note and he and Tam planned to go somewhere. Jason has his driver's license, I'm sure, and probably has a car. What if the note meant whatever they planned to do was all set?" Sam stopped pacing and dropped to sit beside Makayla.

"Then you're saying Tam might be a runaway like the police said?"

Sam shook her head. "I don't think he ran away because he was mad at his dad. I think he made plans to do something."

"But I thought you said Tam wouldn't skip school."

"Well . . ." Sam chewed her bottom lip. Therein was the problem. Tam wasn't the type to skip school. What if he—she snapped her fingers. "He was supposed to meet Darby French before school, beside the building."

"Surely he wouldn't make plans to meet Darby if he knew he was going somewhere, right?" Makayla asked. "So that has to mean he didn't plan to skip school."

"Maybe." It just didn't make sense. There was too much she didn't know and what she did know seemed to conflict with itself. Not a very good combo. Sam sighed. "I don't know."

"And Jason Turner might not be the J.T. from the letter." Makayla shrugged. "That note might not even have anything to do with any of this. That could've been from months ago and Tam just forgot to throw it away. And Jason's in high school, a junior—really past the passing notes stage, wouldn't you say?"

Everything Makayla said was true, but it didn't make

Sam feel any better. She fell back on her bed and stared up at the ceiling. "I wish I knew what the police knew. Like if they found anything on his cell phone, his laptop, or in his room. Or anything else in his locker. Or what he was meeting Darby French for."

"I can't believe you haven't bugged your dad to listen to the scanner or something."

Sam had thought about that, then dismissed the idea. "It usually doesn't have stuff about an investigation. Really only new calls, traffic stops, and stuff like that."

"But if they took Darby French to the station like Marcus suggested, maybe it'll be on the scanner?"

"No." But that gave her an idea. "I'm going to call Marcus and see if he's talked with Darby. I suggested he check in on her."

"Sam Sanderson! You put that boy up to spying for you." Makayla wagged her finger at Sam.

"Not exactly. He was worried about Darby, and I merely suggested he call her after school to see what happened." That wasn't asking him to spy for her.

"And yet you're calling him and going to ask him what Darby said."

"There's nothing wrong with that." Sam knew what her best friend meant, but she was running out of information and leads. She grabbed her cell and the list with all the *Senator Speak* phone numbers, then dialed Marcus's cell number.

"Hi, Sam," he answered. "Have you heard anything about Tam?"

"No. Have you?" She held her breath as she waited for his response.

"I talked to Darby."

She grinned, despite the ugly look Makayla threw her. "What did she say?"

"Well, she did have to go to the sheriff's office with her mom to talk to Deputy Jameson, the one who spoke at our assembly."

"Yeah, I know who he is." She wished he would just get to what she wanted to know.

"She said that when they'd had their regular tutoring session on Tuesday during activity period, he'd asked her to meet him before school."

"Why?" she blurted out. "I mean, did she tell you why he wanted to meet her?"

"That's the strange thing about it all. She says he called her the night before and asked if she could meet him before school, on the side of the building, because he had something he wanted to give her and he needed her to have it before school."

Sam's pulse spiked. "Well, what was it?" She nodded at Makayla, who despite her disapproving look, stared at Sam with great interest.

"Darby doesn't know and since she was late, she never got it."

That didn't sound like Tam at all. A secret meeting

to give Darby French some unknown but important thing and then, what? He disappeared without a trace. "Did you find out why she didn't tell anyone that she'd planned to meet Tam?" Maybe there was a clue there.

"Yeah. Her big brother goes to the high school and drives her to school every morning." The high school is right next door to the middle school, so the two campuses share football and baseball fields. "Their parents' rule is that no one else ride in the car with them, but the brother's apparently been giving his girlfriend a ride to school. Wednesday, when they went to pick up the girlfriend, she'd overslept, so was running really late. Darby couldn't really do anything but wait, because her brother threatened to tell on her for something she did at home that would get her grounded."

Sam shook her head, once again grateful she was an only child. She'd seen firsthand how Makayla's little sister, while cute, could cause problems for Makayla. Now, problems with an older sibling. Yep, Sam was happy being an only child.

Marcus continued. "So, she didn't say anything because she would have had to explain why she was so late, which would get her brother in trouble and that would make him tell on her."

"That's crazy." Yeah, Sam could see going to great measures to not get in trouble, but when a friend was missing? That seemed to be more important than having your brother mad at you and getting grounded.

"Anyway, she and her brother both got in pretty hot water, from what she said, but the police let her go without doing anything else for now."

So Darby was a complete dead end. "She really has no idea what he wanted to give her?" Makayla's stare stayed glued on her.

"She says she doesn't," insisted Marcus.

"It's very unlike Tam to break routine. He's just not one for spontaneity. At least, not that I've noticed."

"That's what Darby said. That it was very unlike him. That's why she was so upset to be late."

But not upset enough to come forward when she heard he was missing. "It just doesn't make sense."

"I know. That's what Darby keeps saying."

Sam had had just about enough about Miss No-Help Darby. "Well, I'm glad at least the police have something new to go on. Tam broke his own routine, and for someone to do that there's usually a significant reason."

Makayla tilted her head. Sam shook her head.

"Darby said they kept asking her who J.T. was. She doesn't know a J.T. so didn't have an answer for them. What's up with that?" Marcus said.

"I guess that's an angle the police are working." Sam knew better than to share information she'd gotten that she wasn't supposed to have access to. Yep, she'd learned that the hard way. "Did she say they asked her anything else?" Maybe there was another lead in this dead end some other way.

"Well," Marcus hesitated for a long moment before continuing. "She said they asked her if she knew anything about the teen message board *teenmeetLR* or anything about anyone who goes by the screen name of *tutorcool* or *mathhater*."

"Why would they ask that?" What did a message board have to do with Tam?

"She said the cop who interviewed her wouldn't say." Marcus paused. "But, Sam, why would they ask Darby if it didn't relate to Tam?"

"I don't know. What board again?"

"*TeenmeetLR*. I've never heard of it, have you?"

Sam's dad tapped on the door, then pushed it open. "Dinner's ready, girls."

She nodded as he backed out. "Marcus, I have to go. Thanks for filling me in."

"I hope they have something to go on to find Tam," Marcus said.

"Me, too. Talk to you later, Marcus." Sam hung up and stared at her best friend. She was more confused than ever about Tam, what he'd been up to, and where he'd been.

She was more worried about him now too.

CHAPTER NINE

"Hey, Dad, do you know anything about a local message board called *teenmeetLR*?" Sam asked as she shook red pepper flakes onto her pizza. Dad was, after all, one of the Little Rock detectives who rotated service on the Internet safety task force.

He'd just taken a sip of water and nearly spewed it all over the kitchen table. He swallowed and coughed before he answered. "Where did you hear about that message board?"

Ahh . . . she'd hit on something. A message board that Dad apparently knew about and, by the red creeping up the side of his face, one he didn't like.

"From a friend of a friend." Which was true. Darby was a friend of Tam's and Marcus's, and they were her friends. That didn't stop Makayla from throwing her a sharp look.

"You need to stay out of there." Dad's face turned into his bulldog look—eyebrows drawn down, lips puckered tight. His cheeks even seemed to sink in and turn red. "Both of you—don't ever go there, and tell all your friends to stay out too."

His reaction sent every alarm bell off in Sam's head. Loudly.

"I'm serious, Sam. This is non-negotiable."

"We'll stay out, Mr. Sanderson," Makayla said, her eyes wide. "We'll tell everyone to stay away too."

"Yeah, Dad," Sam managed to eek out, even though she was still stunned by his reaction. *TeenmeetLR* must be bad, very bad.

"Honey?" Even Mom sounded concerned about his reaction.

"I'm sorry, it's just that the task force has been monitoring that particular message board for several weeks now and what they've found is not good."

"What do you mean, Dad?" Because there had to be a connection between the board and Tam, or the sheriff's deputy wouldn't have asked Darby about it. "Bad how?"

Dad slowly set his pizza on his plate. "They've linked at least two child predators to that specific location. One has already been arrested by an undercover team, but the other one, they haven't been able to catch yet."

Sam's heart slipped to her toes. The pizza seemed to churn in her stomach.

"You haven't been in there, have you, Sam?" Dad asked.

She shook her head, unable to speak because her tongue felt five sizes too big.

"Have you, Makayla?" Sam's mom asked.

"No, ma'am."

"Then why do you look so pale, Sam?" Dad stared hard at her, so hard she wanted to squirm.

She had the worst taste in her mouth that almost made her sick, and for once, she couldn't keep information for her story and not share it with her father. This was about Tam and it could be linked to his disappearance. "Dad, the deputy working Tam's case asked someone about that message board and two specific screen names. I guess maybe they're connected."

"What are the screen names?" The way the lines around Dad's eyes deepened . . . his entire expression was weighted in concern.

"A *mathhater* and *tutorcool*. Do you know anything about them?"

If possible, his face paled by a whole other shade. Or two.

"Dad?"

He shook his head. "I don't recognize the name *mathhater*."

Sam's tongue felt raw like the time she'd taken a sip of her hot chocolate before it cooled. "How could they think this relates to Tam? His screen name is *Tamaton*.

He can't be *mathhater*, Dad. Tam's super smart, especially in math." It just didn't make sense.

"I don't know, Sam."

"What about *tutorcool*? Do you recognize that screen name?" she asked.

He glanced at her mom.

"Dad, come on. I'm trusting you with information I found out. Isn't that what you wanted me to do—bring important stuff directly to you?" She needed to know about this. It was that important.

Her mom looked at her dad. "She has a point." Mom smiled at Sam and Makayla, then looked back at Sam's dad. "They're mature enough to understand."

He sighed and ran a hand down his face. "The other predator we've been looking at is *tutorcool*."

Fear lodged in the back of her throat, but she forced her voice to remain steady. "A predator in what way?"

"He's been on that board and a few others, talking to kids by posing as a college freshman who tutors middle and high school kids." Dad's voice sounded squeaky almost, not as steady and calm like usual.

"But he isn't?" Makayla asked.

"Not hardly. As best as the task force can determine, he's in his late thirties or early forties, probably divorced and has employment. The profile built on him is that he possibly works night security someplace. His tracked activity online seems to be late afternoon to early evening, when middle grade kids are online."

"Aside from lying about being older than he really is, what does he do that's so bad?" Sam needed to know. If Tam was possibly connected to this guy . . . *God, please don't let Tam be involved with him.*

Dad sighed and stared at Sam's mom. She gave a little nod of her head. Dad sighed again. "We believe he is responsible for the attempted abduction of three children in the surrounding area."

"How old are the kids?" Makayla asked.

"All are in middle school. A sixth grader and two seventh graders."

Same age as them. Sam wanted to throw up. "Did he kidnap them?"

"No. But he tried."

"Dad, tell me." Tears burned the back of Sam's eyelids, but she didn't care. She'd come this far, she needed to know the truth. *God, please not Tam. Please don't let Tam be with this bad man.*

"Independently, this guy attempted to abduct three boys. According to the boys' reports, they met this guy on the message board, talking about tutoring."

"Wouldn't the parents have been involved with tutoring?" Sam's mother asked.

Dad shook his head. "All three had gotten in trouble for their grades in math, so they sought out someone to help them without their parents knowing."

Sam nodded, not trusting herself to speak. She could understand a kid wanting to bring up their grades without telling their parents about a tutor. But this couldn't apply to Tam. He certainly wouldn't need tutoring. He *was* a tutor. Maybe the deputy was way off base. She met Makayla's stare and recognized the fear mirrored in her eyes. Tam couldn't be involved with this guy.

Dad continued. "Even with the information from the boys, the unit hasn't been able to find the man."

"So he's still out there, preying on kids?" Sam was almost afraid to ask, but she had to. She had to know.

"Yes." Dad's voice sounded tight.

"And the police are pretty sure this *tutorcool* is responsible for the kidnapping attempts?" Makayla asked, her voice a much higher pitch than usual.

Dad took a sip of his water. "They think it's one possibility. There are many other possibilities in that case, from what I understand."

Sam took a drink of her water, ignoring her pizza. She couldn't have eaten anything now even if she were starving. "Dad, can you find out if they think Tam was on that message board and has a connection to *tutor-cool*? Please. They had to ask for a reason and I'm really worried." Scared out of her mind was more like it, but she wasn't going to go there right now. She couldn't. If she let her imagination start with this . . . well, there was no telling where it all would end.

He frowned. "Pumpkin, I know you're worried about your friend, but—"

"Charles, what would it hurt for you just to see if Tam's name is listed on anything having to do with that message board or user? It's not like you're interfering in anyone's investigation." Sam's mom balled her napkin tightly and set it on top of her half-eaten piece of pizza.

Sam chewed the inside of her bottom lip.

"I'll see what I can find out." Dad looked at Sam. "I won't be able to tell you much, even if I look into it. And what I do find out, you cannot print or post. Understand?"

Sam nodded. "Yes, sir."

Dad stood and carried his paper plate to the trash. "I'll let you know after I talk to some of the other task force detectives."

Jumping up, Sam rushed over and hugged her father. Hard. "Thanks, Dad. I love you."

He kissed the top of her head. "I love you, too, pumpkin. Now, why don't you and Makayla go ahead and get your showers out of the way? You do have school tomorrow."

"Yes, sir." Sam turned to Makayla. "You go ahead and go first. I'll help Mom clean up, then take Chewy out."

Makayla nodded and handed her plate to Sam, then headed toward Sam's room.

"Thanks, Mom, for getting Dad to look into it for me."

Sam's mom put pizza from the box into a plastic container. "I know you're worried about your friend, Sam. This is more than just investigative reporting. This is personal because it involves someone you know and like. This is when being a reporter gets tough."

"What do you mean?" Sam threw the paper products away and grabbed the dish towel.

"Reporting on something when it involves someone you care about . . . it's hard to remain objective. Neutral. To report the facts." Sam's mother sealed the container and stuck it in the refrigerator. "It's tough when your own emotions are in play."

"I need to write an article about the assembly today. I just don't know what to say." Sam opened the door for the dog. Chewy darted outside into the evening, barking at a squirrel that scurried up a tree. "Everybody at school was at the assembly so they heard it all firsthand. Not too much of a scoop there."

"Look at it from a different angle. Was there something that was hinted at, but not announced? Something maybe you could explain?"

"Not really. They didn't talk about too much. They just confirmed Tam was missing, which I'd already posted on the school's blog, and asked for everyone to write something on the index cards." Sam went on to explain to her mother the process that happened during the assembly. "Now, I did learn something after the fact," Sam admitted.

Mom raised her left eyebrow. "Do tell."

Sam leaned against the counter and told her mother about the note. "But I guess I can't mention that, huh?"

"That depends . . . were you told not to mention anything about what you saw or heard in the office?"

"No, ma'am." Sam started to feel a spark of excitement burning in her chest.

"Did the deputy realize that you saw the note?"

Sam remembered the ugly look he'd given her, then how he'd snatched up the note. "I'm pretty certain."

"And even after he realized you saw it, he didn't tell you not to say anything?"

"No, ma'am."

"Did he know you were with the press?"

"Well . . . I asked Mrs. Trees for more information for the school paper right in front of the deputies."

Mom pressed her lips together until they formed a tight line.

Sam smiled. "You think it's okay for me to print about it, don't you?"

"I can't tell you how to investigate or report, Sam." But Mom smiled.

"Thanks, Mom." Sam really appreciated how Mom helped her see all the sides to reporting, but left the decision on how to do it up to Sam.

"Sam." Mom tilted her head toward the kitchen door. "Chewy wants back in."

"Thanks." Sam opened the door and let Chewy back inside.

"And feed the cat."

Sam resisted groaning and did as her mother asked,

using the time to let her mind begin to form the article she'd write. Maybe she wouldn't reveal exactly what was written in the note, just hint at it. Feed the suspense and make people anxious to read the next article she wrote.

She bounded into her room where a pajama-clad Makayla sat in front of her makeup mirror applying face cream. "Got a lot to tell you, but let me take a quick shower first." Sam grabbed her clothes from her top drawer.

"Okay, but hurry," Makayla said.

In less than fifteen minutes, Sam stood in her room, using a towel to rub over her wet hair, and relayed her conversation with her mother to her best friend.

"Well, it's a good thing your mom kinda let you know it was okay, because you know when you print anything about that note, Mrs. Trees is going to have a hissy fit." Makayla carefully braided her hair for bed.

Sam laughed, despite the circumstances. "What, exactly, is a hissy fit? I mean, everyone always says that, but I've never seen one."

"Just watch Mrs. Trees when she reads your article."

Sam laughed, but knew exactly what her best friend meant. "I just can't imagine Tam visiting Internet locations that aren't monitored by trusted adults. He helped build the safe list we posted on the school's blog." Sam plopped down on the foot of her bed, her oversize comb in her hand. Her mind was as matted as her hair. When wet, the long, dark brown strands looked almost black. "It just makes no sense."

"I know." Makayla turned and faced Sam. "I'm not going to lie, Sam, I'm scared for Tam. Especially after hearing what your dad told us."

"Me, too." Sam moved to her desk and accessed the school's newspaper blog entry page. "That's why it's so important to get as much information out as soon as we can. To see if there are any leads." She began typing up the article she'd written in her mind during her shower.

—This reporter has it on good authority that Tam Lee had a secret meeting planned with a certain student on the day he went missing. Sound Off, Senators: if you were the student set to meet Tam, or know anything about it, you're encouraged to contact the Pulaski County Sheriff's Office immediately. ~Sam Sanderson, reporting

"Sam?" Dad knocked on her bedroom door.

"Yes, sir?" Sam plopped onto her bed beside Makayla.

He stepped in the doorway and leaned against the doorframe, Mom beside him with her arm around his waist. "They've issued an AMBER Alert for Tam." Dad's face was grim. "It was just on the news."

Sam felt sick again. "So they finally believe he's not a runaway?"

"They're covering all the angles." It was what he didn't say that made Sam's stomach tighten like the first time she rode the X-Coaster at Magic Springs.

"What about that message board, Dad?"

He pulled out her desk chair and took a seat. Mom joined Sam and Makayla on the bed. "I talked to the task force supervisor. Sam, this is totally off the record. I mean it, not even a hint of what I'm about to tell you. It is an open, ongoing investigation and right now, it is critical not to say anything. Understand?"

"Yes, sir."

He nodded. "They tracked Tam's online history on his computer. Tuesday, he went into the site under the name *mathhater*. He had one conversation with *cooltutor* that was recorded, but they couldn't find a private chat between them."

Tears burned the back of Sam's eyes, but she couldn't cry in front of her father. He'd never shared so much information with her before, and she would not allow her emotions to make him regret it. Nor would she betray his trust and write about this.

But she was terrified. "What does that mean?"

"It means the task force is working to get the identity of the predator confirmed and bring him in."

"Do they think Tam met with him?" Makayla asked, the fear very obvious in the shaking of her voice.

Sam's mom took one of each of the girls' hands and squeezed.

"They truly don't think so, but Tam did have contact with him. With Tam's disappearance they have to treat it as if he could have. I'm so sorry."

Makayla sniffed.

"Girls, let's pray together for Tam, okay?" Sam's mother said.

They bowed their heads, and Sam's mother prayed for Tam's safety and quick return. Yet Sam remained as confused as ever.

And even more scared than before.

CHAPTER TEN

"I want you to do something for me, Mac." Sam had thought about this since her parents left her room. She knew Makayla wouldn't like it, but Sam was desperate.

"What?"

"I want you to hack into Tam's Facebook account."

"You've got to be kidding. There's no way." Makayla stared at Sam, then sighed. "You're serious. Why?"

"I want to see if he has any private messages with Jason Turner. If they've communicated, I want to know about it."

"Don't you think they could've texted or called? Emailed even?"

"But I can't check those. Facebook we can. And since it's not something the police have in their possession, like his cell phone or laptop, you won't get into trouble for hacking in." Well, at least, in her mind that's how it should work. She truly didn't know for sure. "Please, Mac. I'm looking for anything that could've happened to him besides . . . well, I just can't think of a single logical reason Tam would've been on that board under that screen name."

Makayla nodded. "I was thinking about that too. I wonder if maybe he loaned his laptop to someone and they're the ones who went into the board."

Sam snapped her fingers. "That could be why they asked Darby." She nodded. That made sense. "Because Tam was tutoring her in math, they probably wondered if she was the one using his laptop."

"Or someone else. For all we know, he could've been tutoring several people." Makayla flashed the first genuine smile since dinner.

"Of course, the police would still have to look into the predator, but Dad did say it was just *one* conversation. That could've been when Tam let someone borrow his laptop."

The smile reached Makayla's eyes. "I bet that's it."

"Still," Sam said, "we need to check his Facebook account. If the message board is a dead end, then we're still no closer to figuring out where Tam is. Even if there isn't a private message from Justin, maybe there's something there that would give us a clue."

"Us?" Makayla shook her head. "Oh, no, Sam. I'm not hacking and prying to give you dirt for a story."

"It's not just for a story, Mac. I'm really worried about Tam." That stung, that her best friend in the whole wide world would think she was more concerned about a story than her friend.

"I didn't mean that. I'm sorry." Makayla reached over and squeezed Sam's hand. "I'm just stressed and scared and worried. Tam and I aren't friends, but if he can just go missing, then it could just as easily be me or you or my little sister or anybody."

Sam nodded and squeezed Makayla's hand back. "I know. That's why I'm trying to figure this all out. Yes, I want to write a story, a story that will help bring Tam home. But more than that, I want to be able to write the story of his safe homecoming."

Makayla stood and stretched, then sat in front of the desk. "I'm not sure I can hack into the messenger program, but I can try to hack his Facebook account and go to his private messages that way."

Sam refrained from letting out a whoop and dancing around the room. She bent down to run her fingers over BabyKitty's soft fur. The cat stayed curled up on the foot of the bed, her tail twitching every now and again.

Makayla went to Facebook, then to Tam's page. "Since Tam's such a computer whiz, I might not be able to hack into his account at all, but since it was set up a couple of years ago, maybe . . . just maybe I'll catch a break."

Sam watched as Makayla went into computer ninja mode. In seconds, she'd gone into a black screen Sam had never seen before. She sat up to watch her best friend a little closer.

"It'd be easier if I had some of my programs, but I think this might be my way in." Her fingers flew over the keyboard, tips of nails tapping on the keys.

It all looked foreign to Sam, almost like a DOS prompt or something. She was lost, but Mac flipped through screen after screen, typing in strings of random code like the wicked mad whiz she was.

"I think I've—rats, blocked." Makayla talked more to herself than Sam. "Let me try this way. I've gotten in this way before on another program."

The room was silent except for the sound of the tapping of keys and Chewy snoring in her dog bed beside the desk.

"Boogers! Hmm." Makayla paused, staring at the monitor. "Maybe . . ." Her fingers went back to typing.

Sam wanted to pace, but she didn't want to disturb Mac's progress. She closed her eyes and laid her head back against the headboard.

What was she missing? There had to be something.

She pulled out her smartphone and opened the notes app, then began listing the facts as she knew them. She started with the timeline:

—Tuesday during activity period, Tam asked Darby French to meet him before school on Wednesday, on the side of the building, because he wanted to give her something, but she says she has no idea what that was.

—Sometime Tuesday, since Sam's dad didn't say, someone on Tam's laptop went into a message board under the screen name *mathhater* and had a conversation with *cooltutor.* This might or might not have been Tam, but Sam was leaning toward it not.

—Tuesday night, Tam got into an argument with his parents about spending the night at Luke Jensen's. He posted about the disagreement on Facebook, but Luke said he sounded more disappointed than angry at his father.

—Wednesday morning at seven fifty, Tam's mother dropped him off at the school.

—At an unknown date, someone named J.T. wrote Tam a note that said everything was set for in the morning.

Sam reread the notes she'd typed. In her mind, Darby was off the hook. The police had already questioned her and determined she didn't know anything. She never got whatever it was Tam wanted to give her because she was late showing up, so Sam figured she knew nothing else.

The message board still didn't feel like it was something Tam would do. It just wasn't logical, and Tam was always so precise and purposeful. For him to go—

"I'm in!" Makayla's excitement broke through Sam's thoughts.

Sam bolted off the bed, sending BabyKitty to her feet with her ears laid back. Even Chewy jumped up from her bed and gave a low growl.

"Sorry, pets." Sam hovered behind Makayla, squeezing her shoulders. "I knew you could do it. So, does he have a private conversation with Jason Turner?"

"Let's see." Makayla scrolled through all the inbox messages so fast Sam couldn't keep up with all the names.

"I'm not seeing one," Makayla said.

"Scroll slower. I don't know how you can read any of that as fast as you're going."

Makayla shook her head, but she slowed down. She went up and down through the list twice. "Nothing here."

Sam collapsed back onto the bed. She'd been so hopeful.

"I'm sorry," Makayla said. "Hey, we tried."

Sam sat upright. "Did he have any private messages on Wednesday?"

"Let me check. Um. No. Well, not that he answered." Makayla shrugged. "There are a lot of them later in the evening from people messaging him to ask if he's okay."

"What about Tuesday?" Maybe there was still something useful. Sam hated to waste a hack.

"Um. Let's see. There's his and Luke's conversation

about Tam not being able to go to Luke's and Luke asking if he was okay."

"Hang on, let me see." Sam scrolled slower as she read.

"This feels like we're spying. It feels wrong," Makayla said.

Sam felt that way, too, but she needed to find something—some other lead she could use to help find Tam. "There's nothing else for Tuesday." Disappointment tightened in her chest.

"I'm going to go ahead and back out of his account," Makayla said.

Sam put her hand over her best friend's. "Wait. Let's check all last week's messages, just to make sure there isn't something else we're unaware of."

"Okay, but you look. It's making me feel like an eavesdropper." Makayla stood and petted the cat.

Sam didn't take offense to the fact that she was an accomplished eavesdropper. Mom had told her that sometimes being a careful listener took a story in a new direction. The right direction.

Tam didn't have a lot of private conversations. One with Marcus about an upcoming story and letting Marcus know what he needed photographed, since Marcus was the paper's photographer. Another conversation with Lin thanking him for the flower. Wait . . . flower? Sam knew she shouldn't, knew that the conversation had nothing to do with Tam's disappearance, but she read the conversation. Lin, a fellow cheerleader who had made homecoming court and asked Tam to escort her, sent Tam a private message almost a week ago to thank him for the flower he put in her locker. Aww, how sweet.

"Come on, Sam. You're just snooping now." Makayla tapped on the footboard of the bed.

"Hang on, just a second." Sam closed that conversation and went back to looking. Nothing interesting jumped out at her. "Okay. How do I get out of here?"

Makayla moved toward the keyboard, but before she could touch a key, the private message screen popped up from somebody named *Anon*.

Tam?

Makayla jumped as if her hand had been slapped. "*Ohmygummybears*! What do we do?"

"I don't know." Sam's hands were frozen over the keys.

Tam? Where are you? Are you okay?

"Sam, we're going to be in trouble." Makayla sounded like she wanted to cry.

"Just hang on." Sam held her bottom lip between her teeth. She hesitated for just one more minute before she typed a response.

Who is this?

"Sam!"

"Shh. Let's just see."

Tam Lee? Is that really you?

Sam stared at the blinking cursor. She typed again.

Who is this?

The reply came across the screen.

Who is *this*?

"Sam, what if it's that predator or somebody like that? We need to sign off." Panic rose in Makayla's voice.

But this was the only lead Sam had.

I asked first. Who is this?

This isn't Tam. Who is this?

"Sam, please." Makayla had tears in her eyes.

"Just one more second." Sam hovered over the screen name. Instead of giving the little box of info like usual, it was blacked out. Now Sam's pulse raced in panic. "Okay. You're right. Get us out of here."

"Finally." Makayla took over the keyboard and with two clicks and one string of code, the screen went blank for a moment, then back to Sam's desktop. Makayla let out a burst of air, then collapsed onto the bed. "Don't. Ever. Do. That. To. Me. Again." She sat up and stared at Sam. "Ever!" She sounded like she'd just finished one of her karate tournaments.

"Sorry." But Sam found herself a little out of breath as well.

"Who do you think that was?" Makayla asked.

"I don't know. I've never seen that black out of information before. Have you?"

Makayla shook her head. "It's almost . . . creepy. Like someone knew we were in Tam's account." She shuddered. "Okay, I might not know what I want to be when I grow up, but I can assure you, a spy isn't one of them."

The mental image of Makayla creeping around in her karate uniform broke the tension and made Sam laugh out loud.

"What?" Makayla wanted to know.

"You take karate and are awesome at it, but you are so non-confrontational it's not even funny."

Makayla sat still for a moment, as if trying to decide whether to be offended or not, then joined Sam in the laughter.

Then guilt over laughing when Tam was missing sobered Sam right up. "I just wonder." She went to Facebook, signed into her account, and opened a search for *Anon*. Nothing came up. "That's so strange."

"I know. It creeps me out."

"Yeah." Not only did it creep her out, it really bothered her. It was as though someone knew they were in Tam's account . . . and Sam didn't like that. She typed in Tam's name, brought up his page, then clicked on his list of friends.

"What are you doing now?" Makayla asked.

"I'm going to send Jason Turner a message." She clicked on his name, then on "Send a message."

"What are you going to say?"

Sam shrugged. "I'm just going to ask him if he

remembers Tam." She typed, *Hi, Jason. I think I might have met you at the EAST conference last year in Hot Springs. Are you going again this year?* Then she hit send.

"You didn't mention Tam," Makayla said.

"No. I'm just starting a conversation. If he has nothing to do with Tam's disappearance, he should ask about him, or at least mention him." That was logical, right?

"Oh. Maybe."

"It's better than nothing." Because as of right now, Sam had no other ideas.

CHAPTER ELEVEN

Sam!" Mom hissed.

She rolled over in bed and put her arm over her face, covering her eyes from the light spilling in from the hallway. Sam groaned.

"Samantha!"

That got her attention. She sat up, rubbing her eyes. "What's wrong?"

"You girls need to get up and put on robes. The sheriff's deputies are here to talk to you both." Mom sounded more than a little angry.

"What's going on?" Sam blinked to read the time on the clock on her bedside table. Midnight? "Is it Tam?" Had they found him? *God, please let him be okay.* She couldn't think of a single good reason to be woken up just hours after they'd gone to bed.

"Just hurry. Both of you." Mom snapped her fingers

and pointed at Chewy. "Stay," she commanded the dog before she shut the door behind her, plunging Sam's bedroom into darkness once again.

Sam jumped out of bed and woke Makayla, who resisted being awakened just as much, if not more, than Sam. In minutes, they were pulling fluffy robes over their pajamas and squirming into socks.

"Your mom didn't say what it was about?" Makayla whispered.

"No, but it has to be about Tam, right?" Sam whispered back, not sure why she was whispering when it was just the two of them in her room.

Makayla froze as she stood. "What if it's about my parents and sister?"

Sam's heart stuttered. Some friend she was—that it could be Makayla's family hadn't even occurred to her.

"Hurry up," Makayla rushed her.

The sock rolled again as Sam tried to jam her foot into it. Forget it! "Come on, let's go." Sam grabbed Mac's hand and they headed into the living room.

All three lamps were on. Mom and Dad sat side-by-side on the couch, both wearing their sweats and looks of irritation. Deputy Jameson sat in the chair across from the couch. He looked as grumpy as BabyKitty when it was time for her flea and tick treatment. Standing behind him, hovering like a creepy butler in a popular anime show, was Deputy Malone.

Everyone turned to look at them as they walked into

the room. Sam felt like she'd just stepped under a giant microscope. Makayla squeezed her hand.

"Girls, sit down." Dad motioned to the couch beside him.

Sam sat next to him, Makayla on her other side.

"The deputy here has some interesting information about Tam." No mistaking the hint of sarcasm in her father's voice. That wasn't good. Dad wasn't the sarcastic type. So when he resorted to it . . .

Makayla let out a long breath. Sam squeezed her hand. Her family was fine.

"We've been monitoring Tam Lee's email and texts and his social media sites," Deputy Jameson said.

Sam's heart went freefalling to her toes. She felt Makayla go rigid beside her.

The deputy nodded. "By your expressions, I believe you've answered my question. Did one of you hack into Tam Lee's Facebook account tonight?"

Makayla gasped quietly under her breath. No way could Sam let her take the heat for this. Not when Sam had pushed her.

"Yes, sir." Sam held up her chin, meeting the deputy's cold stare. She didn't exactly say she'd done the hacking, she just answered the question. That wasn't lying. Wasn't even really misleading. If they assumed she'd done the actual hacking, that was okay. She had a feeling they didn't care so much who actually did the deed.

"Why would you do that?" Dad interrupted to ask.

Sam glanced at her father, then her mother. "Because I was hoping there'd be some sort of private message exchange with someone that would give me a clue to where he is." Her mom's lips were nothing more than a thin line under her nose.

"Oh, Sam." No mistaking the disappointment in Dad's voice. A grounding was sure to come soon, but she couldn't worry about that right now.

"Anyone in particular?" Deputy Malone stepped out of the shadows and stared down at Sam.

"I, um, actually hoped to find a conversation between Tam and Jason Turner." Sam could sense Makayla deflating beside her with every passing second.

The two deputies looked at each other, then back at her. "Why Jason Turner?" Deputy Jameson asked.

Sam shrugged. "Because his initials are J.T. like in the note."

"I see." Deputy Jameson pinned her with a look that sent the hairs on the back of Sam's neck to full attention. "And that's why you didn't respond when contacted to chat?"

"That was you?" Makayla blurted out.

Deputy Jameson nodded. "We've had Tam's accounts under constant monitoring. As soon as someone was in his account, we began tracking it." He glared at Sam. "Imagine my surprise when the IP trace led me here, where a detective lives."

Dad shifted on the couch beside Sam. Oh, yeah. No question about it, she was in the doghouse for sure.

"So you can be assured that Tam isn't hiding out here." Dad's voice was back to being calm and steady, but Sam could hear the hint of irritation in his voice.

"I'm sure." Deputy Jameson flipped his stare from Sam to Makayla, back to Sam, then Makayla again. "I would think the child of a detective would know that hacking into someone else's account is illegal, as is interfering with a police investigation."

Sam could feel both her father and Makayla stiffening. "I'm really sorry," Sam started. "I just felt like maybe I could help in some way."

"As if we are incapable of doing our jobs, and a seventh grader could do it better?" Deputy Jameson asked.

"You hadn't issued an AMBER Alert. You treated it more like Tam was a runaway, even though everyone told you he wasn't." Sam's hands shook. She curled them into balls and set them in her lap.

"There are many ways an investigation is run, and I'm not inclined to discuss my methods with a kid." No mistaking the irritation in his voice now.

"She understands that, Deputy, but you can clearly see how it looks to those outside law enforcement, not just children," Sam's mother said, using her interview voice.

Sam wanted to air fist through the living room, but

thought better of it. Dad was already annoyed with her and, truth be told, he had every right to be.

"I think we've taken enough of your time," Deputy Malone said.

Sam's parents stood.

Deputy Malone held his hand out to Sam's father. "Thank you for helping us clear up this matter." He nodded at Sam's mother.

Deputy Jameson didn't say anything, just turned and marched to the front door.

Sam's mom locked the front door behind them then faced the girls.

"Mom, Dad, I'm sorry. Really. I just thought maybe they hadn't thought to look through Tam's Facebook closely because they thought he was a runaway. Well, until the message board thing came up."

"Mr. Sanderson, I'm the one who actually did the hacking," Makayla said.

"I figured, but we know who pushed you to do it."

"Dad, I'm just worried about my friend and trying to help figure out what happened to him."

"Sam." Dad's tone left no room for argument. "You know better. We'll discuss your behavior and the consequences tomorrow. Right now, you girls get to bed. You have school in the morning."

"Yes, sir," they said in unison.

"Goodnight, girls," Sam's mom called after them.

Sam shut her bedroom door and tossed her robe

onto the back of her desk chair. "I'm sorry, Mac." Her dad was already mad at her, she certainly didn't want her bestie upset with her too. She bent to pet Chewy, whose whole body was wiggling.

"No, it's okay. I knew it was wrong but did it anyway." Makayla shrugged. "I'm just glad to know the pop-up chat was the police."

"Yeah. Me too." Sam waited until Makayla had gotten situated before she turned off the light. "But I'm sorry for getting you involved. Dad's going to give it to me tomorrow, that's for sure. I'll probably be grounded."

"You know what, Sam?"

Sam yawned. "What?"

"Well, just wait until he sees your post in the morning. That'll really upset him."

Oh, boy.

CHAPTER TWELVE

"*Samantha!*" Aubrey's shrill voice rose above the normal sounds of the kids in the cafeteria before school on Friday.

Sam gritted her teeth and turned to face the she-beast, as Lana liked to call her. "Yes, Aubrey?"

"Ms. Pape and Mrs. Trees want to see you in the office. Right now." By her gleeful tone and expression, Sam was sure they weren't happy with her.

"On my way." Sam turned to Makayla. "I'll talk to you later. Keep your ears open in case someone mentions Tam." She rushed to the office, then stood outside for a moment to slow her breathing. She let out a long breath, then pulled open the door.

"Ah, Sam. Mrs. Trees said to send you right back to her office," Mrs. Darrington said.

Sam nodded and headed down the hallway. It had

to be about her article, but really, it wasn't so bad. She hadn't mentioned the note, nor had she mentioned anyone by name or even initials. She'd kept to the facts. Really, there wasn't much they could get upset with her about.

She knocked on the principal's door, then pushed it open when Mrs. Trees said, "Come in."

"You wanted to see me?" Sam asked, trying to smile at Ms. Pape, who wouldn't meet Sam's eye.

"Sit down, please, Sam," Mrs. Trees said.

It was only then that she noticed a girl sitting in a chair almost in the corner.

"This is Darby French, Sam. She's most upset, you see." Mrs. Trees looked at the girl, who had clearly been crying. "Why don't you explain, Darby?"

"Look, I know you know I was supposed to meet with Tam the day he disappeared because Marcus told me that he told you." Darby French sounded angry.

"Um, okay." Sam didn't see her point.

"So why would you post that article? I've already told the police everything I know, and you know it. Marcus said you called him and he told you everything." Darby's bottom lip protruded a little. If she wasn't pouting, she was missing a perfect opportunity.

"You think the article was about you?" Sam shook her head.

"Who else could it be about? Everybody keeps telling me I need to come clean, but I already have."

"Darby, the meeting I mentioned wasn't about you at all," Sam said.

"Then who?" Mrs. Trees asked.

Uh-oh. Now she had to tell the principal she'd been referring to the note, and Mrs. Trees was apt to, as Makayla put it, have a hissy fit.

"Well, Sam, if you weren't referring to Darby, what were you referring to?" Mrs. Trees probed.

"I have it on good authority that it's possible Tam had something else planned the morning he disappeared." There, she could say that much.

"You're sure you weren't implying me?" Darby asked.

"I'm positive."

"Darby, go on back to the cafeteria now," Mrs. Trees said.

"Yes, ma'am. Thank you." Darby shot Sam a quick look before disappearing out of the office.

"Okay, Sam, tell me what you meant," Mrs. Trees said.

Well, the principal would find out eventually. "I was referring to the note found in Tam's locker."

"What note?" Ms. Pape sat up straight in her chair.

"Yes, Sam, what note?" Mrs. Trees asked, but her eyes reflected that she knew exactly what note Sam was talking about. Was she asking to see if Sam would lie to her? Sam had never lied to Mrs. Trees.

Misled, possibly. Avoided answering, most definitely.

"Sam?" The principal wasn't going to let her slip out of this one.

"The note found in Tam's locker. The one that said everything was set for in the morning. The note signed by someone named J.T." Sam blurted it all out so fast that her words almost tumbled on top of each other.

"How do you know about the note?" Mrs. Trees asked.

"I saw it. It was lying on the table in the conference room before Deputy Jameson picked it up."

"You were snooping?" Mrs. Trees took off her reading glasses and set them on her desk.

"It was lying on the table, right out in the open. I didn't go looking for it." True. She was already where it was, she'd just had to work to get a better view of it. "It wasn't like I was digging through drawers or something."

"Because it was lying in the office, you thought it would be okay to read and use the information as you saw fit?" Clearly, the principal was not amused.

"I just . . ." Sam shook her head. "I'm sorry, Mrs. Trees. I saw the note, couldn't help but read it, and since I'm worried about Tam, I posted the article. I thought it would be okay because I don't actually mention the note itself, or who it's signed by. I wasn't revealing anything that would hinder the investigation in any way." She let out a breath.

Everything she'd said was true. This was probably the first time she'd gone out of her way to keep so many facts secret. Usually she posted everything in her articles, but this time . . . well, she was more worried about Tam than anything else.

Mrs. Trees stared at her. Sam remained silent, holding the principal's gaze. She'd done the best she could, but she couldn't help thinking if the police had acted faster . . .

The tardy bell rang loudly, signaling the beginning of the school day.

"I can appreciate your concerns for your friend, Sam, and I do appreciate how you didn't actually mention the note or the name." Mrs. Trees lifted her reading glasses and tapped the end of the earpiece against her chin. "Ms. Pape, what are your thoughts?"

Ms. Pape visibly jumped in her seat. "What?"

"Your thoughts?"

"Oh. Well, I believe that Sam, acting as a journalist, used the information she believed to be reliable. She used it in a manner that didn't reveal too much, nor did she mislead the public. She requested anyone with information to contact the authorities. In my opinion, her intent was clear and she should be commended for her reporting."

Sam's breath caught. Never before had the paper's faculty sponsor shown such out-and-out support for Sam.

Mrs. Trees paused for what seemed like a handful of minutes, again tapping the earpiece on her chin to some erratic beat no one else could hear, then shoved the glasses back on her face. "Very well, then. You are free to go to class, Sam. Mrs. Darrington will give you a pass."

Sam retrieved her pass from the school secretary, rushed to her locker, and headed toward her first period, English. She handed the pass to Mrs. Beach and took her seat, right behind Grace Brannon.

A few minutes after Mrs. Beach started the lesson, Grace turned to Sam. "Hey, Sam?"

"Hey." Sam looked at her friend and fellow cheerleader.

Grace glanced over her shoulder to the teacher then leaned down closer to Sam's desk. "Did you know my uncle does freelance work for local law enforcement?" she asked.

"No." Interesting, but Sam couldn't imagine why Grace was telling her this.

"He was over for dinner last night and told my mom about an interesting case he's been working on this week."

Sam didn't know what to say, so she just nodded and listened with half an ear, the other half trying to pay attention to Mrs. Beach's instructions for their classwork for the day, a worksheet on sentence diagramming.

"He told Mom that he'd been going through the cell phone of a kid the police thought had run away. He was going through the phone to report text messages and history of the browser and stuff, apparently because he could do it so much quicker than the regular IT group with the sheriff's office."

That got Sam's undivided attention. "Tam's?" Sam leaned forward in her seat.

"He didn't know whose it was, and I didn't want him and my mom to realize I was listening to their conversation when I was supposed to be cleaning the kitchen, but it sounded like it."

Sam glanced at Mrs. Beach as the teacher handed the front row students stacks of handouts to take one and pass back, then whispered to Grace, "Why did you think it was Tam's?"

"Because my uncle said he was surprised that there were a lot of security codes and stuff installed on a junior high kid's phone. But more importantly, he said he found a deleted text message conversation between the phone's owner and someone named Lin where he told her not to worry if she heard something about him. He said everything was okay and she'd understand later." Grace turned and took the last two papers. She set one on her desk and handed the other to Sam.

Sam's mind reeled as she took the worksheet.

"I knew right away it was Tam's because he and Lin have been getting to know each other. At least, that's what Lin told me when we had our cheerleading pictures taken."

And he'd given Lin a flower in her locker. It had to

be Tam's phone! "Are you sure he told Lin not to worry? That everything was okay and she'd understand later?"

Grace nodded. "That's exactly what my uncle said."

"What else did he say?"

"Nothing that I heard. He and my mom went to sit out on the porch, so I couldn't hear any more of their conversation."

"Did your uncle happen to say what the dates were of the text messages?" Sam asked. Man, would she like to talk to Grace's uncle.

Grace shook her head. "He didn't say exactly, but he said he'd been pulling the information off the phone from the past two weeks, so it had to be during that time. At least, I would think."

"Thanks." Sam sat back in her seat, staring at the worksheet but not seeing it at all.

Why hadn't Lin come forward? The assembly . . . the article . . . surely she had to know everyone was worried sick about Tam. Why hadn't she said anything? What else did she know that she hadn't told anyone?

The cafeteria was packed to capacity as Sam wormed her way through all the students in line for hot lunches. She looked around until she found Makayla sitting with Felicia. She joined them, dropping her lunch bag on the table. "What a crazy day it's been."

"Started early too," Makayla said. "Hurry up and bless the food so you can tell me what happened with Mrs. Trees this morning."

"Dear Lord, thank you for the food we're about to eat. Please use it for the nourishment of our bodies and our bodies to bring honor and glory to You. Amen." Sam opened her bag and pulled out her bottle of water. "It's all good. I'm still in shock that Ms. Pape stood up for me, though." She took a sip then proceeded to tell them about her morning in the office.

"Wow, that's cool, do-gooder," Felicia said. "It's about time she stood up for you instead of always backing you-know-who every time we turn around."

"That is cool, unlike last night." Makayla chomped on the Cheetos Sam's mom had gotten especially for Makayla to make her lunch. "Think your dad is going to ground you?"

"I'm sure."

"What'd you do?" Felicia asked.

While Makayla explained, Sam searched the lunch tables. It was possible Lin had first lunch, but maybe not. Although, at the moment, Sam didn't see—wait, there she was. Sam took a gulp from her water bottle. "I'll be right back," she said to no one in particular and headed toward Lin.

Lin sat with Remy Tucker, another cheerleader, and Thomas Murphy. She smiled as Sam approached. "Hi, Sam."

"Hey. Can I talk to you for a second, Lin?"

"Sure." Lin stood. She and Sam stood off by the wall. "What's up?"

"I'm not trying to be nosy, but I'm worried about Tam. Are you?" Sam studied every blink of Lin's eye and every muscle movement of her face.

"I'm very worried. It's not like Tam at all. I know the police think he's run away, but I just can't believe that." Nothing showed on Lin's face except worry.

"Do you think the police still believe he just ran away?" Sam pushed.

Lin nodded, then moved closer to Sam. "I'm not supposed to say anything, but the police came by to talk to me yesterday after school."

"They did?" Sam hadn't heard anything about this. Then again, why would she? She truly detested that the case wasn't in her father's jurisdiction.

"They had somebody go through Tam's phone and found a conversation he and I had a week ago. Because of how it sounded, they wanted to know what it was about."

Sam glanced over to where Makayla and Felicia stared at her from across the cafeteria. "Was it suspicious or something?"

"Nothing like that. He just wanted to tell me that if I heard something about him, not to worry."

Just as Grace said her uncle had said. Sam crossed her arms over her chest. "That does sound a bit like he was telling you not to worry if his missing was made public."

Lin nodded. "That's what the police thought, but once I explained everything, they realized they were wrong."

Curiosity nearly choked Sam. "What was that?"

"Well . . ." Lin's cheeks turned bright pink. "I know you know that I've had a crush on Tam and that we'd started talking to get to know each other better. Right?"

Sam nodded. But that had happened like a month or so ago.

"A couple of weeks ago, Tam started tutoring a girl in math. She's really pretty and sweet, and some of the guys saw Tam tutoring her during activity period."

Right. Darby French. She was really pretty.

Lin continued, "They started picking on him about having a crush on her and that's why he was tutoring her. It isn't true, of course, but you know how guys can be."

"Childish," Sam said.

Lin grinned. "Exactly. Anyway, Tam had texted me one afternoon because some of the eighth grade boys had told a lot of people that Tam had a crush on her." The pinkness deepened and brightened in her cheeks. "Tam didn't want it to get back to me and hurt my feelings. I mean, we're just friends and everything, but . . . yeah."

It did make sense now. "Oh. I get it."

"Yeah, when one or two of the guys really made a point of picking on him right in front of me when we were walking to newspaper together, he felt so bad that the next day, he put a flower in my locker." Lin smiled, and blushed even more. "How sweet is that, right?"

Sam grinned. "Very sweet."

"So, have you heard anything about him being missing? I've been worried sick, but right now, I don't think there's much we can do except pray for him." The blush had disappeared from Lin's face, replaced with an expression of worry.

"I know. I'm hoping that now that the AMBER Alert is issued, there will be more action to look for him."

"I heard that a couple of churches were getting together to make meals for Mr. and Mrs. Lee and do some chores for them. My mom is one of the organizers. She says that Mr. Lee has had to keep going to work even though Tam is missing, because he's a surgeon and he saves lives."

"That has to be hard: saving other children's lives when your own kid is missing." Sam couldn't even begin to imagine how she'd feel if she were Mr. Lee. Oh, the irony.

"Well, I'd better get back to lunch before the bell rings," Lin said.

"Yeah. Me too. Thanks, Lin." Sam rushed back to her table. She'd barely had enough time, in between bites of her peanut butter and jelly sandwich, to tell Makayla and Felicia about the text messages and what Lin told her, before the bell rang.

As she headed to her locker, Sam couldn't help but think that no matter what she did or which way she turned, every lead was a dead end.

CHAPTER THIRTEEN

Sam sat at a table in newspaper. Aubrey had already flitted by several times, hinting that she'd finished the design for the paper's new masthead. She went out of her way to be obvious, making a point to "secretly" show only certain people the new design—people in her clique that she liked.

As if Sam cared. She sat in front of her monitor, staring at the blinking cursor, listening to Felicia and Lana on either side of her chat as they wrote their articles to turn in to the she-beast. Sam knew she needed to write a new article, but so far, all she had was the news that Tam's disappearance had apparently been upgraded enough for an AMBER Alert to be issued.

Such dire news.

"Hey, Sam." Jared Hopkins slowly approached the girls' table as if they would pounce on him at any given moment. He'd hit his growth spurt early, so stood almost six feet tall, even though he was in the seventh grade too. He had dark brown hair and eyes, and mainly kept to himself. Jared seemed like a textbook introvert, so Sam had always wondered a bit why he was on the newspaper staff.

"Hi, Jared."

He kept his head ducked. "Uh, can I talk to you for a minute? Alone, maybe?"

"Sure." Sam stood and moved away from the girls, standing almost in the corner of the room.

Jared faced her, standing close. "I know where Tam went Wednesday morning. His secret meeting."

"What?" Every muscle in Sam's body went rigid.

Jared's face turned red. "He left school after his mom dropped him off and came to my house."

Shut up! "What?" Sam knew she sounded like a parrot, unable to speak except to repeat the same word again, but it was all her mind could force out. "I didn't know you two were close friends." Questions jumbled in her mind, and none of them was making sense.

"We aren't. Not really. We hang out here and in science, but that's about it. Look, he came to me and said he just needed to place to hang out for a day, during school hours, and he knew I lived close by and my parents work all day." Jared shrugged. "It wasn't a big deal, so I told him he could hang at my house."

"Let me get this straight . . ." Sam's mind couldn't

process what she was hearing. "Tam *planned* to skip school and went to your house? To just hang out?" This was crazy. Jared had to just be messing with her. Aubrey probably put him up to leading her on. She glanced over to where Aubrey stayed in her idea of paradise, holding court with Kevin Haynes' full attention.

Jared nodded. "I live right on Chalamont Drive, just behind the school's baseball field, so we just met on the blacktop of the school at eight o'clock that morning, walked to the house, and I let him in. Then I came back to school."

"This was all *planned*?" She couldn't swallow that. "You're kidding, right?" She glanced over to where Nikki Cole had joined Aubrey and Kevin Haynes, as well as some of the other eighth graders on the paper's staff. All of them were totally ignoring Jared and Sam.

"About two weeks ago, Tam and I were talking, and he asked if I knew a place where he could hide out for just one school day. I could tell he was hinting, so I offered my house." Jared shrugged. "I've let friends do it before."

"Y'all talked about this two weeks ago?" Sam couldn't believe what she was hearing. What was Tam up to?

"About then, give or take a day or so. Then, he put a note in my locker on Tuesday to reply with a note in his locker if it was all still okay for him to come over on Wednesday morning, so I did."

The mysterious note. Now its meaning made perfect sense. Sam nodded. "You're J.T."

Jared gave her a funny stare. "How'd you know?"

"I know about the note."

His eyes widened. "Tam told you?"

"No, I saw the note. The police have it. They're trying to figure out who J.T. is." She frowned. "Hold up . . . your last name is Hopkins."

He grinned. "Jared Thomas Hopkins, Junior. My mom calls me J.T. since she calls Dad Jared." He stopped smiling. "Wait a minute. The police have my note?"

Ohmygummybears! She couldn't believe this. "So where's Tam now?"

"I don't know." Jared looked like he'd just swallowed a bug.

"What do you mean, you don't know? He hung out at your house. Where did he say he was going when he left?"

"That's just it: I never saw him that afternoon. When I got home from school, he was gone. He'd cleaned up after himself like I'd asked, so there was no trace of him. There wasn't any sign of him."

"Where did you go after school?" Sam asked.

"I didn't go anywhere. I went straight home from school and when I got there, he wasn't. I figured he'd just left early or decided to 'fess up and went home to tell his parents."

Sam shifted her weight from one leg to the other. This was getting more and more crazy by the minute. "What was the original plan?"

"We'd talked about how my mom gets home from work around five and my dad gets home a little after that, so they'd just assume he came home from school with me for dinner."

"Your parents let you just have friends over without getting permission first?"

"I do it all the time. Don't you?" Jared asked.

"Uh, no." Her mom was extremely lenient when it came to friendships, but even she wouldn't be thrilled if Sam just had someone over without asking first. Unless it was an emergency or something.

"Oh." He gave her an *I feel sorry for you* look, that she chose to ignore.

"Anyway, the plan was for Tam to have dinner with you and your family?" Sam struggled to get back on track with the story even though she struggled with accepting it. All of it was so totally un-Tam-like.

Dad was so right: you can never really know somebody. She would've never thought Tam capable of this.

Jared nodded. "We were going to have dinner with my parents and then Tam and I were going to do homework. His plan was to head home by ten. He said that would give him more than enough leeway for the three hours."

"The three hours?"

"Yeah, I don't know what that was about. He just said he'd call his mom a little before ten and she'd come get him."

"Even though he had skipped school and made her worry?" Sam couldn't get the mental image of Mrs. Lee in the office, wringing her hands with worry over her missing son, out of her mind. Her respect for Tam dropped several levels. Putting his mother through such agony. In the back of Sam's mind, she couldn't help but wonder if this was all still some big hoax on her. "If he skipped school, he wouldn't have had any homework to do."

"I guess. He said he needed to work on his EAST project."

Wasn't that the truth?

There was so much about Tam that she'd had wrong. She'd thought him responsible and considerate, someone who wouldn't skip school or ask for secret meetings or who wouldn't have an important part of their project done. There was nothing in his EAST project files and only random data in Mrs. Shine's. Facts on tween Internet stats. Missing children and how the first three hours—wait a minute!

Sam grabbed Jared's forearm. "Three hours? You're positive Tam said three hours?"

Jared nodded. "Yeah. I thought it was odd because school gets out just before four, so from then until almost ten is double that: six hours."

Unless he was allowing time for his mother to realize he was really missing and call the police.

Surely he wouldn't have gone so far? She let go of Jared's arm, gripping her own upper arms as she crossed her arms over her chest. "But once you saw my article and then went to the assembly with the deputies and knew Tam was missing, why didn't you come forward with all this?"

"First off, Tam had made me promise not to say anything until he explained everything. How am I supposed to know if this isn't all part of his plan?"

"What?" Had Jared lost his mind? "How could being missing be part of his plan?"

"What if he had plans to go to someone else's house?"

"Then why make plans to eat dinner with you?" she volleyed back.

"Maybe something came up and that's why he left early."

No, she thought she'd figured out what Tam had been up to, and that didn't fit. "I don't think so."

"He was supposed to meet Darby that morning. Maybe he'd planned something else and since she didn't show, that changed his plans."

Maybe. "But he's been gone so much longer than planned now. All day Wednesday, Wednesday night, Thursday and Thursday night, and now all day today. That's way longer than he'd intended. Why not tell everyone now, especially since they've issued the AMBER Alert."

"That's why I'm telling you now."

"Have you told your parents or the police?" Sam

asked. How could he not have come forward? Tam had deviated from the plan and had been missing three days and two nights. What had Jared been thinking?

Jared widened his eyes and gave her a hard stare. "Really? You think I'm just going to walk up to the police and announce my friend ran away and I helped hide him? Seriously?" He shook his head. "I don't know if that's a rule violation or something, but I'm pretty certain Mrs. Trees would have me on her watch list if she knew I'd helped someone skip school. And that's not even going into how much trouble I'd be in with my parents."

Sam recalled how the deputies had acted at her house at midnight . . . he had a valid concern. But Tam's disappearance was more important. "Well, you've got to tell them now."

Jared shook his head. "I can't."

"Jared, you have to."

"I came to you, Sam, because I figured you might be able to figure out what Tam was up to. And since your dad's a cop and all . . . I can't get into any more trouble. I'm already seriously grounded until spring break. If I mess up before spring break, my parents said we'd cancel our vacation to Disney."

A vacation over the safety of a friend? Sam wanted to be indignant, but knew in her heart, if the friend wasn't Makayla, she might hesitate coming clean too.

"I have to break it to them gently—in a way they'll understand I was just being a friend." Jared looked more nervous than BabyKitty when Chewy wanted to play. "I have to talk to my mom first. She'll help me break it to Dad."

"Let me think for a minute." Okay . . . considering everything she knew now, she needed to write it all down. Look at it. *See* the connections, as her mother had taught her. "Look, I'll try to buy you some time so you can tell your mom first. I'll keep your name out of it for now, but you have to tell them today. I won't be able to not tell the police. I'll stall them as long as I can."

Once she figured things out.

"Thanks, Sam." Jared hustled back over to sit beside Paul Moore. He glanced back over his shoulder at her and smiled.

Sam returned to her station.

"What was up with that?" Felicia asked.

"Hang on." Sam pulled out her cell phone, mentally thanking Ms. Pape for allowing them to use their smart-phones in class.

She pulled up the notes she'd made last night and added in what she now knew to be the facts:

—Two weeks or so ago, Tam asked Jared if he could hang out at his place while he skipped school. (Sam still had the hardest time with this fact. There had to be a reason, a good one. There just *had* to be.) They made plans not only for Tam to hide out there all day, but to stay until almost ten that evening. (Again, this was the part that Sam had the hardest time accepting.)

—Tuesday during activity period, Tam asked Darby French to meet him before school on Wednesday, on the side of the building, because he wanted to give her something, but she says she has no idea what that was.

—Tuesday, Tam put a note in Jared's locker to confirm whether everything was set for him to go to Jared's house on Wednesday morning. Since it was, Jared put a note in Tam's locker that said everything was set for the morning.

—Sometime Tuesday, since Sam's dad didn't say, someone on Tam's laptop went into a message board under the screen name *mathhater* and had a conversation with *cooltutor*. This might or might not have been Tam, but Sam was leaning toward not.

—Tuesday night, Tam got in an argument with his parents about spending the night at Luke Jensen's. He posted about the disagreement on Facebook, but Luke said he sounded more disappointed than angry with his father.

—Wednesday morning at seven fifty, Tam's mother dropped him off at school.

—Wednesday morning about eight, Jared took Tam to his house and let him in. He told Tam to pick up after himself and he'd be back after school.

—Wednesday after school, Jared returned home and Tam was gone, leaving no note or anything. He'd just disappeared. Jared had no way of knowing when Tam left, where he went, or what was going on at this point.

Felicia looked over her shoulder and read. Sam didn't try to stop her. It wouldn't really do any good to say anything at this point since Felicia was a speed reader and was probably already finished anyway.

Sam looked back over her notes, trying to remember everything. There was something she was missing . . . the three hours! She needed to see exactly what Mrs. Shine's notes in her EAST documents were. There was an explanation there, Sam just had to find it.

CHAPTER FOURTEEN

Mrs. Shine!" Sam burst into the EAST lab.

All the students and Mrs. Shine looked up. "Sam, what can I help you with?" Mrs. Shine motioned Sam to approach her desk.

"I need to look at your documents for Tam's project. I think his disappearance might be connected to his project."

Mrs. Shine accessed her documents. "Students, keep working," she said to her class. "What's going on?" she whispered to Sam.

"I went into Tam's files to see what he was working on."

"Sam." Mrs. Shine tried to sound disappointed, but it didn't quite work. Everyone knew Sam was Mrs. Shine's star student.

"All his files are empty, Mrs. Shine. All of them. There's nothing there."

"That can't be." Mrs. Shine opened her file.

"I double checked. I'm positive."

"Let's see what I have in my notes." She clicked on Tam's name. "Well, there's not much. Let me print it."

Sam grabbed the paper as soon as the printer spit it out. She read aloud in a whisper. "Awareness to possible danger is critical to the safety of children. Awareness of physical surroundings, potentially suspect people, and Internet safety measures should all be integral teachings to children." She glanced at Mrs. Shine. "Approximately eight hundred thousand children under the age of eighteen were reported missing, of that, more than two hundred thousand were abducted by family members. Ninety-three percent of teens, ages twelve to seventeen, use the Internet, eighty percent use it over three times a week. The first **three hours** are the most critical when trying to locate a missing child."

Sam's hands shook as she held the paper. "Mrs. Shine, Tam's disappearance *is* his project."

"Explain, Sam."

She showed the teacher her notes on her phone. "Tam was proving his point for his project—that there is a need for a mandatory safety education for all students of upper elementary school. He did the research and I would bet he has an entire project nearly complete, just not on the school's servers. He didn't want anyone to figure it out before he proved his point."

"I think perhaps we should take this to Mrs. Trees."

Sam nodded, but her mind kept racing. "I'll meet you at the office after school, okay? I need to go get my stuff from the newspaper room."

"Okay."

Checking the time on her phone, she realized she needed to move. She walked as quickly as possible to the classroom then went directly to her station.

"What is going on, do-gooder?" Felicia asked.

"Hang on. I've got to get the article up before school lets out." Sam looked over the monitor to see Aubrey staring at her. Sam dropped her head behind the computer screen. "Y'all keep Aubrey busy, please."

"My pleasure," Felicia said, standing up. "Hey, Aubrey . . ." she started as she walked across the classroom. Lana followed her closely.

Sam opened up the posting program and began to type. The article title: "Where Is Tam Lee?" Her first sentence would grab everyone's attention: *Did he go too far to prove his project's point?*

Her typing increased as she let the story explode out of her. How Tam carefully planned. How he followed through. The meeting with Darby was the only thing she left out, because she didn't see the connection. She mentioned visiting a "questionable" message board to set up the basis of Internet security. She mentioned he deliberately had words with his dad over a long-standing family rule he couldn't break, then posted it on Facebook so everyone would know, making his disappearance seem like running away. She told of his plan to stay at a friend's house, even though she did leave Jared's name out, it was only a matter of time before someone figured it out and he was busted.

She was careful to put in the journalist code words like *allegedly, a source reveals*, etc., but the gist of Tam's project was there.

The bell rang. Sam typed faster to finish up.

—Sound Off, Senators. If you know where Tam went after leaving his friend's house on Chalamont Drive, call the police immediately. How far would *you* go to prove a point in your school project? ~Sam Sanderson, reporting

She didn't have time to reread it because Aubrey was fast approaching. Sam hit the SEND button, then closed the program and grabbed her backpack.

"What are you doing, *Samantha*?"

"Sorry, Aubrey, can't stay to let you try and bother me with your attitude. I have an appointment with the principal and Mrs. Shine." She smiled and hiked the backpack up on her shoulder.

"Getting in trouble in other classes too?" Aubrey was so snide sometimes.

Sam shook her head, turned around, and marched

out of the classroom. There were just times when not responding was a much better option.

She remembered to text her mother to let her know she'd be late coming out, then went into the office.

"What do you need this time, Sam?" Mrs. Darrington sounded tired of her.

"Mrs. Shine and I need to speak to Mrs. Trees."

"Really?"

"Yes, ma'am. Mrs. Shine is meeting me here after her class clears."

"There's nothing on Mrs. Trees' schedule about a meeting."

"It's unplanned, but I'm pretty sure she'll want to talk to us."

The office door opened and Mrs. Shine stepped inside. "Good, you're here, Sam." She smiled at Mrs. Darrington. "We need to speak with Mrs. Trees. It's very important."

The school secretary looked at Sam. "So I'm told. Just a moment." She lifted the phone, turning her back to them.

"I looked it all over after you left. I think you might have something, Sam," Mrs. Shine said.

Sam nodded as her pulse raced. Finally. Something.

"You can go on back to her office," Mrs. Darrington said, replacing the phone onto its cradle.

"Thank you," Mrs. Shine said as she led Sam down the hallway.

The principal's office door was open. "Come on in," she said as they approached. "What's going on?"

Mrs. Shine took a seat, while Sam sat in the chair beside her. "Sam's got a theory about Tam Lee's disappearance that I believe has merit. Quite a bit of merit, actually." She smiled at Sam. "Why don't you bring Mrs. Trees up to speed with what you've learned and your theory?"

Sam began talking, laying out the facts as she knew them and how they connected with each other and Tam's project. As she spoke, she noticed the principal nodding. Finally, Sam had explained everything as best as she could.

"Well, that's some theory." Mrs. Trees spun her reading glasses around by the earpiece. "I think it's probably a good idea to have the deputy working Tam's case come to the school to hear this theory." She lifted the receiver and dialed.

Sam looked at Mrs. Shine. "I texted my mom that I'd be late coming out. Maybe I should go get her to come in, so she isn't outside waiting."

Mrs. Shine nodded. "I'll let Mrs. Trees know as soon as she gets off the phone."

Lifting her backpack, Sam slipped out of the office and into the breezeway then headed to the parking lot. Mom's car sat parked on the front row. Sam opened the passenger door and tossed her backpack in the backseat.

"Hey, my girl. How was your day?"

"Eventful. Listen, can you come inside? I think we're waiting for the deputies from last night to get here."

Her mother frowned. "Whatever for?"

Quickly, Sam told her mother what she'd learned and pieced together. "So Mrs. Trees called them while I came out here to get you."

"Well, let's get in there." Her mom locked up the car, sticking her cell phone and keys into her purse. She wrapped her arm around Sam's shoulders. "I'm really proud of you for sticking with the facts and uncovering everything. That shows great reporter instincts."

Sam practically floated back into the office.

And right into the harsh glare of Mrs. Trees who waited in the reception area for her.

"Sam Sanderson, why on earth would you post that article?" the principal asked.

Deflated, Sam ignored the ringing of the phone. "Wh-what do you mean?"

"You posted an article stating your theory." Mrs. Trees looked as if her head might explode at any given moment.

"You said the theory had merit enough to call the deputies." Sam stood a little straighter with her mother beside her.

"What seems to be the problem?" Sam's mother asked.

"Your daughter posted an article with her theory of Tam's disappearance."

Mom nodded. "It's probably a theory that will be proven sooner rather than later."

The phones continued to wail, despite Mrs. Darrington's continuous answering.

"Do you hear that?" Mrs. Trees asked, but it was clearly a rhetorical question since she didn't wait for an answer. "Parents are calling wanting to know if our administration condones a child faking their own disappearance for a project. They want to know if any teacher had the information and just didn't tell anyone." She shook her head. "It's a madhouse, and it's all your fault." She glared at Sam.

"Actually, she just reported it." Mom turned to Sam. "You did post that this was your theory, right?"

Sam nodded. "I made sure I wrote that it was allegedly what he did and I didn't mention the actual ch—er, anything I'm not supposed to. I made sure to state that sources revealed, but I didn't name anyone's name except Tam's."

"Then I think she's within her right as a reporter," Sam's mother told the principal.

Sam wanted to fist bump her mom, but figured that would be a bad idea.

Mrs. Trees frowned that deep, drag-down-her-entire-face frown and gave a curt nod toward her office. "The deputies are on their way. Why don't you two go wait in the conference room with Mrs. Shine until we can get the phone situation under control?"

Sam led her mother to the conference room.

"Sam, let me see the article. Can you pull it up on your phone?" her mother asked.

"Yes, ma'am." She quickly pulled up the school newspaper's blog and handed her phone to her mother.

Her mother scrolled then handed the phone back to Sam. "You might have jumped the gun just a little in mentioning that Tam deliberately posted on a questionable message board to establish a possible Internet security problem, but the rest of it looks fine to me."

Sam hugged her mom and exhaled slowly.

"It'll be okay, my girl."

"I'm glad you picked me up instead of Dad."

Mom stopped her from walking into the conference room and turned Sam to face her. "Sam, you have to know that Dad's always on your side. He's just required to color a little more inside the lines than I am. Don't ever doubt that your father has your back." She smiled and kissed Sam's forehead. "He's always got both of our backs."

"I love you, Mom."

"I love you, too." Her mom took her hand and stepped into the conference room. "Hello, Jenny," she greeted Mrs. Shine.

"Hi, Joy. How are you?"

Sam sat down as her mother and her favorite teacher chitchatted. Mom could say what she wanted, but when other cops were involved, Dad had to color all the way inside the lines.

Besides, he was already miffed at her because of the Facebook hacking. Maybe if she solved the case, he wouldn't ground her until high school.

"Well, now," Mrs. Trees walked back into the room, carrying a bottled water. "Would anyone else like some water?"

Both Mrs. Shine and Sam's mother declined. Sam wanted some, but figured she ought not push the principal too much more. It looked like Mrs. Trees had about reached her limit. She sat at the head of the conference table and drank her water in silence, like she refused to say anything until the police arrived.

She didn't have to wait more than five minutes before the door to the conference room creaked open and deputies Jameson and Malone entered.

"So, we meet again, Mrs. Sanderson," Deputy Jameson said as he took a seat in the chair across the table from Sam's mother.

"So we do. And this time in the light of day. So much better."

Sam bit her tongue not to outright laugh at her mother's sarcasm despite her sickeningly sweet tone of voice.

"I understand you have some information regarding Tam Lee's disappearance?" Deputy Malone addressed Sam.

"Yes, sir," she replied.

"Can you tell me everything? Please don't leave anything out." Deputy Malone sounded so much nicer than Deputy Jameson. He laid a small notebook on the table and pulled a pen out of his pocket.

"Let me use my notes, okay?" Suddenly, Sam felt very nervous.

"Of course." Deputy Malone smiled.

Sam was really glad her mother sat beside her in the stuffy conference room. She was pretty sure Mrs. Trees and Deputy Jameson would eat her alive if her mother wasn't there like a mama bear protecting her cub.

Slowly, Sam read her notes on the facts of the case, pausing to expound when needed, and answer any questions the deputies asked. The main hiccup came when she talked about Tam going to Jared's house, although she refused to give his name.

That was a problem.

"Sam, you know you have to give us the name of this friend," Deputy Malone said.

She shook her head. "I can't. I don't have permission to share that information just yet. He needs time to tell his parents."

"Like they aren't going to learn about this?" Deputy Jameson chimed in.

Sam glared at him, a sense of bravado in her since Mom was right beside her. "He wants time to tell them first. I can understand he needs to be the one they hear it from."

"But we need to speak to his parents," Deputy Malone said softly. "While this friend might not have seen any traces of Tam or a clue to where he went, it's possible his parents may have noticed something minor that was off. Something they wrote off as unimportant, but once they know what happened, they might recall." He lowered his voice a little more and leaned in closer to her. "The longer this goes on, the more likely they are not to remember some minor thing that could be the very clue that leads us to Tam."

Sam nodded. "I know. I'll tell you his name, as soon as he lets me know it's okay to do so. I can't give up my source without permission."

"You're a middle school kid, girl. I don't think you have real sources," Deputy Jameson said.

"Oh, quite the contrary," Sam's mother interrupted. "Just because you don't like what she has to say doesn't mean what she's saying isn't right."

"Do tell." Deputy Jameson dripped sarcasm more than Chewy drooled over bacon.

Sam's mother crossed her arms and rested them on the table, then leaned forward and narrowed her eyes as she spoke to the deputy. "The last time I checked, Arkansas still had the reporter's privilege protection as well as many shield laws. Not only are these safeguards in place to assist national and state reporters, they are also there to protect college, high school, and middle school newspaper reporters from giving up their sources of information. I understand you're doing your job, I do, because my husband is a detective. Sam said she would turn over the name, but that doesn't mean you need to bully her. She's giving you information that you haven't been able to uncover on your own."

Man, Sam loved it when her mother went all journalist on people. Deputy Jameson looked like he'd been hit across the head.

Sam's mother turned to face Sam. "Having said that, Sam, a child's life is in the balance and I don't believe any reporter should withhold information about a missing child."

Sam felt sick to her stomach. It did all come back to Tam. She'd been so wrapped up in watching her mother defend her rights as a reporter, she forgot Tam was still missing. "Hang on. Let me text him quickly to tell him I'm about to give his name." Without waiting for any type of response from anyone, she bolted into the hall.

After sending Jared a quick text that simply read: *I'm having to give up your name. For Tam's sake. Hope you've had time to tell your parents.* Then Sam went back into the conference room and took a deep breath before she said, "Jared Hopkins."

CHAPTER FIFTEEN

I'm sorry, Mom," Sam said as soon as they were in the car and heading home.

"For what?" Sam's mother kept her eyes on the road.

Sam shrugged, even though her mother wasn't looking at her. "For making you come into the office and defend my reporting. I should've just given them Jared's name as soon as he told me. I wasn't thinking."

"Oh, my girl, you have so much to learn, but your heart is always in the right place. I'm so proud of you for today."

"Really?"

Her mother flashed Sam a quick smile and nodded. "Of course. I told you it's hard to balance reporting when your emotions are involved. You made a very hard and grown-up decision to tell your source you would buy him time to inform his parents. But you did give up your source to help find Tam. That's was a hard call to make, but I believe you made the right one. I'm very proud of you." She reached over and squeezed Sam's shoulder.

Sam felt as if a ton of weight had fallen off her shoulders. She couldn't wait to call Makayla and tell her everything. She planned to do just that as they pulled into the garage and her mom shut the door behind them. But they'd barely stepped into the house when Dad met them in the hallway.

His face was red. His eyebrows scrunched to where they almost formed one single line. He did not look happy.

"What's wrong?" Sam's mother asked as she hung her purse on the peg.

"I just got a call from Captain York," Dad started.

Sam chewed the inside of her bottom lip. Dad's captain could be quite nasty. His son, who went to school with Sam, wasn't much better, only he was more of a whiner than nasty.

"About?" Mom's voice didn't waver as she wove her arm around his waist and fell into step with him walking down the hall.

"About a certain someone posting an article that tells the world Tam staged his own disappearance, which encourages other kids to do the same thing. News reporters have been hounding the sheriff's office ever since, and because the reporter was my daughter, they called my boss, telling him to talk to me about her."

Mom led Dad into the kitchen where she pulled two bottles of water out of the fridge and handed one to Sam. "Well, they shouldn't have done that."

"But they did." He turned to Sam. "Why would you do that?"

"Whoa, honey. Did you read the article your daughter wrote?" Sam's mother asked, setting down her water and pulling her cell phone from her pocket.

"Um, no." Dad glanced at Sam, not looking nearly as angry as before.

"I'm so proud of her." Sam's mother handed him the cell phone.

Dad scrolled, reading, then handed the phone back to Sam's mother. "It's well written, Sam."

Mom shook her head. "Charles! Yes, it's well written, but it's also good reporting."

"That's not the point."

"Then what is the point?"

Sam stayed silent. Her parents didn't argue, but they sure had some lively debates. Sam had learned that during these times, it was best for her to adhere to the old saying: do not speak unless spoken to.

"The point is she revealed that the whole thing was planned. A setup, if you will. That a kid orchestrated his own disappearance."

Mom shrugged, using her hands for more emphasis.

"She reported the facts as they are right now. She didn't reveal anything she shouldn't have, nor anything she gave her word she wouldn't mention. She protected her sources to the public. That's good, clean reporting, Charles." She popped her hands on her hips. "I'm so proud."

"Of course you are," he mumbled.

But it was loud enough that Sam's mother heard it. "What do you mean by that?"

"Just that you are looking at it from a reporter's perspective. I have to look at it from a cop's." He groaned.

Mom softened her tone. "What did your captain say?"

"You mean after he chewed me up one side and down the other? Telling me how tired he was of having my daughter disrupt an investigation—"

"Dad, I didn't disrupt anything," Sam forgot her vow to remain silent. "They still wouldn't have a clue that Tam did this all for a project if I hadn't written the article about secret meetings. Jared wouldn't have said anything to anyone, and the sheriff's office wouldn't have any idea where Tam had gone. At least now they know where he went from school and that he went willingly and wasn't abducted." She stopped talking because she ran out of breath as though she'd just finished the cheer team's long program.

"But you don't know for a fact that Tam did all this for a project," he argued.

"Yes, yes I do." Sam stood up straight. "I know Tam Lee. I know what kind of person he is. He would allow this to happen so he could show kids how important safety and awareness of their surroundings is. He would do this to prove the point that awareness classes needed to be mandatory to help kids protect themselves."

"So where is he now? Putting his parents through so much . . . that doesn't sound like a kid you should be defending, Sam."

"Dad, I know it sounds like he's uncaring, but I *do* know what kind of person Tam is, and some of the things he said to Jared confirm he never intended this to go on so long. His plan was to be home by ten Wednesday night."

"It's now Friday, pumpkin. Why did he leave his friend's? Where did he go?"

"That's what we don't know, Dad, but I can tell you, it's something beyond his control."

"How can you be so sure?" he asked.

"Because I know him. Trust me, Daddy, something's happened. Tam didn't plan on being gone so long, and if he could contact his parents and straighten it out, he would. I know it." She reached out and grabbed his hand. "Please don't write off what I'm saying because I'm a kid. I know Tam."

Sam's father looked at her mother, then back at Sam. "Okay. Captain York said I should do whatever was necessary to help the sheriff's office find the missing boy and restore a semblance of order in the community."

"You mean, you get to help in the investigation?" Sam's body jumped with excitement. This was perfect!

"Sam, calm down." Dad's voice went stern.

She stared at the kitchen floor, hoping she looked contrite because she certainly didn't feel that way.

"Now, as I said, Captain York wants the situation handled and soon. I'm to help as needed, but, and here's where I need you to pay close attention, Sam . . ."

She lifted her head and met his stare.

"I'm not to step on the sheriff deputies' toes. This is their case."

"But they aren't doing such a great job, Dad."

"Sam."

She nodded. "Okay. Yes, sir."

"The deputies have called Jared's parents. They were heading over to speak with them and look over the house when Captain York called. I imagine they're there now." He let out a long sigh. "I think the supportive thing for me to do would be to go over there and offer my assistance."

Sam widened her eyes. "Can I go with you?"

He cocked his head to the side. "I know you did not just ask me that."

Hey, it was worth a try, right? "I know, Dad. I had to ask though."

He ran a hand over her head, much like he used to do when she was much younger. "I know, pumpkin. But what I do need is for you to be by your phone. If there's something there that I see or hear that maybe you might be able to explain, I'm going to call. Okay?"

For once, she'd be assisting the police instead of fighting them. Could be interesting. "Of course."

He kissed her forehead, right at her hairline. "I'll get going." He looked at Sam's mom. "Walk me out?"

"Of course." She took his hand as they left the kitchen.

Her parents' affection sometimes made her want to gag, but for the most part, she was happy that her parents were loving with one another. They debated with drive, but they also showed their love with just as much energy and dedication.

Sam quickly sent a text to Makayla and filled her in on everything that had happened. Her phone rang almost immediately.

"Hey, Mac. I can't talk long. Need to keep the line open once Dad gets to Jared's house."

"Sam, have you seen the school's blog?"

She'd been so busy . . . "No, why?"

"*Ohmygummybears*, girl. It's blowing up."

"What do you mean?"

"Just people posting about how they're worried about Tam even more now and some are talking about how we, as a society, put too much emphasis on academic competition and excellence. Oh, and that sparked a lot of posts on the argument of school versus homeschooling, to which you know my mother paid attention."

Sam groaned. Mrs. Ansley had made noise this year, for some strange reason, about how it might be a good idea to homeschool Makayla and her little sister. Makayla had managed to squelch the notion for many months, but it was always there, lurking in the Ansley home, just like a monster from a bad dream. Sam would be miserable if Makayla wasn't at school with her every day.

"There've been over six hundred comments, Sam."

"That's insane." Even the bomb threat at the local theater hadn't gotten that many hits.

"Tell me about it. Parents and students alike are posting. Most of the kids are posting kudos to Tam, which is fueling the parents' comments about how this is such a bad example and how Tam is leading kids astray."

"Oh, that's ridiculous."

"I know, I know. I'm just telling you what the comments consensus is right now."

The door to the garage closed and Chewy ran to the front window, barking as Dad's truck eased down the driveway.

"I've got to go. Keep me posted," Sam told Makayla before hanging up.

"Well, that was fun," Sam's mother told her as she came back inside.

"I'm sorry, Mom, but thanks for sticking up for me."

"No worries, my girl. It's easy to defend when you're on the right side." She smiled. "How about a snack? Dad doesn't seem to think he'll be gone too terribly long, so I don't want to eat something heavy now and ruin dinner."

Sam nodded. "Popcorn?"

Her mom smiled. Hot popcorn with lots of melted butter was Sam's mother's weakness. "I'll get it started."

While they worked in the kitchen, Sam told her mother about Makayla's call.

Her mother smiled. "I'm truly so, so proud of you, Sam. Getting people thinking and talking, that's what reporting is all about."

"But some of their comments aren't really in support of the right stuff, Mom."

Her mom laughed. "Silly girl, that's what discussions are all about—people presenting their own opinions about topics. No two people are the same, so opinions vary. That leads to good conversations, which causes people to think. That's the best goal of any reporter I know."

Sam nodded as the microwave beeped.

"Oh, the awards and accolades are nice, don't get me wrong, but it's pretty awesome when someone tells you that something you've written made them see things in a different light." Mom pulled the popcorn bag from the microwave and replaced it with a cup of butter. She turned it on and dumped the popcorn into the big ceramic bowl they'd decorated together at a local *paint your own* shop. "That's truly rewarding."

The microwave beeped again and Mom poured the melted butter over the popcorn and reached for the salt shaker.

"I guess I never really thought about it like that." Sam grabbed two new water bottles from the fridge.

"Getting a scoop is awesome, and responsible reporting is vital because your reputation is what's on the line, but when you can get people to think and talk and truly consider looking at something from a new angle . . . that, my girl, is the mark of a star reporter." She leaned over and hugged Sam. "Like I said, I'm just so proud."

Sam laughed and grabbed a handful of popcorn. She dropped a piece, and Chewy was there to snatch it up before the five second rule could be debated.

"That dog acts like she hasn't eaten in days," Mom said.

"I know. I think she has to make up for not eating a lot when it's storming. She hardly ate a thing Wednesday night."

"Well, with the tornado sirens going off, I'm sure it hurts her ears." Mom tossed the dog a piece of popcorn.

"Mom!"

Sam's mother laughed. "Poor BabyKitty. She wouldn't even come out from under the couch the whole time the sirens wailed."

"It was a bit scary. I was a little upset to be at school and not home with you."

"I wasn't too happy when we lost power and Internet. Thank goodness I'd saved my piece before the power blipped, and then I didn't think the Internet would ever come back on."

"Speaking of the storm, we're supposed to have some rain tonight. Why don't you take Chewy out and toss the ball or Frisbee around for a few minutes? Just keep your phone in your pocket in case Dad calls."

Sam grabbed another handful of popcorn and snatched up her water bottle. "You just want to keep me out of your popcorn."

Her mother's laughter followed her into the backyard. Chewy ran around, barking at the leaves on the trees and the squirrels running high above her head.

Sam spied the darkening clouds. As she had on Wednesday, she wondered where Tam was, and could only pray he was protected from the weather.

At least they were closer to finding him now than they'd been on Wednesday.

She hoped.

CHAPTER SIXTEEN

I fell into a burning ring—

Sam dug her phone out of her pocket. That was Dad's special ringtone, since he was such a Johnny Cash freak. "Dad?" She slipped back into the house.

Her mom met her at the door.

"Hi, pumpkin. Listen, it's the strangest thing, but Tam's parents just called the sheriff's office and reported Tam had called them."

Sam's throat almost closed. "What? He called them? How? Where is he? Where's he been? What—"

"I don't know all of that. The call was apparently a very bad connection and they got disconnected before he could tell them where he was. We've called the news stations to get the word out that anybody who hears from Tam should please call the sheriff's office immediately. I'm asking you to post the same on your school's blog." There was a pause and rustling sound before Dad continued. "I understand there's a lot of activity on the blog. Maybe your post will help get the word out."

"I'll do it right now, Dad."

"Thanks, Sam. I'll call you if I hear anything." The connection broke.

Sam told her mom what Dad had said as she walked to her bedroom to her MacBook. She quickly typed up a blog post and sent it up. She held her bottom lip between her teeth. "I hope it'll be enough. I hope he can call someone else."

Her mom sat on the edge of the bed and grabbed Sam's hand. "Let's pray." She waited until Sam had bowed her head and closed her eyes, then her words filled the air. "Lord, we ask that You watch over Your son, Tam, just as You've been watching over him since before he was even born. We ask that You bring comfort to his parents, who got to speak to him. We ask that You guide this situation to Your will. In Jesus' precious name we pray, Amen."

Sam felt calmer . . . better. She usually did after she prayed. She leaned over and hugged her mother. "Thanks, Mom."

"Anytime, sweetheart."

"So, what now? We just sit and wait?" Sam stood and started pacing. She thought better when she paced.

"That's about all we can do right now." Her mother stood. "Unless you want to watch a movie on Netflix or something?"

"I don't think I could sit still and pay attention."

"Why don't you call Makayla? Maybe that will distract you." Mom stood at Sam's bedroom door.

"Yeah. Thanks." Sam reached for her cell as her mother walked down the hall.

"Hey, I saw your post. What's going on?" Makayla said as a way of greeting.

Sam quickly told her about her father's call. "And that's all I know right now."

"Mr. Kelly just broke into the regular FOX newscast with the same information. I'm happy he called because that means he's okay, but I'm really worried that he hasn't called back yet."

"I know." That's exactly what was bothering Sam. "I just don't understand how he could call and get disconnected, but not call back. Unless . . ."

"Unless what?" Makayla asked.

Sam decided to go ahead and put a voice to her fears. This was, after all, Makayla, her best friend whom she could share her fears with. "Unless he got away from somebody long enough to make a call, but then the person who took him disconnected the call and hurt Tam or something so he couldn't call back." She realized her heart was thudding, even though she was lying on her back, staring up at her ceiling.

"You have *got* to stop watching whatever it is you watch on television or movies, girl. You are way too dark and scary. Why does your mind automatically go to the super dramatic? Come on, now. You yourself said Tam planned most of his disappearance. Now you're thinking you were wrong and he was kidnapped?"

It did sound a little melodramatic when Makayla said it out loud like that. Okay, a lot over the top.

"I meant after he left Jared's. Seriously. I mean, where is he now? We can only assume he left Jared's Wednesday before school got out, so why hasn't he called someone before now?"

"Maybe he just got access to a phone. Maybe the battery is dead and that's why he can't call back. Maybe it was dead all this time and he just got enough of a charge to call. I don't know, but I don't automatically think this means he's been kidnapped or abducted or something."

"You're right." As usual, Makayla was the voice of reason. "I'm just trying to figure it all out."

Makayla laughed. "And because you can't, it's driving you crazy, isn't it?"

"Are you saying I'm a control freak?" But Sam couldn't stop herself from letting out a giggle.

"Hey, if the shoe fits, lace it up and show it off."

"Tell me you did *not* just use your mother's line on me." Sam gave a little laugh.

"Guilty as charged." Makayla snorted.

"You're just getting ridiculous now." Yet, it felt really good to laugh. Sam felt like all afternoon she'd had a big, heavy boulder sitting in the middle of her chest. Makayla's teasing was like a jackhammer to that rock.

"*Ohmygummybears*!" Makayla's tone sobered Sam immediately.

"What?"

"FOX news just broke through with a live report. It's a reporter, going to Tam's house," Makayla said.

Sam flipped on the television on top of her dresser, quickly selecting the local FOX channel. "I'll call you later."

She tossed her cell phone onto her bed and stared at the events unfolding on the television.

The reporter walked across the walkway to the front door, microphone in hand, cameraman shaking a little to keep up. "We're here at the home of missing child, Tam Lee. FOX has learned from sources close to the case that the missing child called home mere moments ago."

Talk about sensationalizing. This guy made drama queens look humble. Sam sank to the bed and absent-mindedly stroked BabyKitty as she watched, unable to look away.

The reporter rang the doorbell and Mrs. Lee filled the screen.

"Mrs. Lee, I'm Trevor Webster with FOX news. We've been told your son called you? What did he say?" The reporter held the microphone out to Tam's mother.

Sam didn't know what exactly she'd expected, but it wasn't to see Tam's mother standing in her doorway looking so calm and cool, dressed in a cool white pant-suit. Not a hair was out of place and her makeup was flawless.

"My son managed to call me about thirty minutes ago. The connection was very distorted and I could barely hear him. The call ended abruptly before I could find out where he was, but I heard his voice and know that he is alive and okay." Her voice was clear and strong.

Well, if she was Mrs. Lee, Sam guessed she'd be relieved to hear her son's voice and know he was alive, but man, she'd be wanting to know where he was.

"Did he say where he was calling from? Did you check the caller ID?" the reporter asked.

Sam nodded. Good questions, Mr. Eager Beaver.

"*Unknown caller* was what was on the caller ID. I'm sure my son was trying to tell me exactly where he was, but the connection was just so awful."

Sam's mother barged into her room. "Good. You are watching this." She shook her head as she sat beside Sam on the bed.

"I want to thank everyone for their good thoughts and prayers for my family during this trying time. Your kindness is very much appreciated," Mrs. Lee said, smiling into the camera.

"What is she doing?" Sam asked.

Sam's mother laughed, but it wasn't the *ha-ha* laugh. "Some people live for their fifteen minutes of fame, even if it's in the face of tragedy."

"We're very hopeful we'll hear from him again very soon. Thank you." Mrs. Lee shut the door and the reporter turned to the camera.

"This is Trevor Webster, live from Little Rock. Back to you in the studio."

Sam muted the television and faced her mother. "But since Tam called, it isn't a tragedy, right?" She couldn't help but think of her original thought, in spite of Makayla teasing her about being dark and scary.

"It's good that he was okay when he called, but that he hasn't called back . . . well, law enforcement isn't sure what to make of it."

"Have you talked to Dad?"

Sam's mother nodded. "The sheriff's office sent a unit to the Lee residence to monitor any incoming calls. They got there before the news crew arrived."

"But?"

Her mom shrugged. "The longer it goes from the time Tam called—makes them believe the phone Tam used is broken."

"Mom, Tam is pretty good at piecing things together. Computers, tablets, phones . . . maybe it is a broken phone and he's had to fix it by piecing it together. That would explain the bad connection and abrupt end. If he's still trying to get it to work again . . ."

"That's why they sent the unit from Jared's house to Tam's. To be there just in case he calls again."

"Did Dad say how it was going at Jared's?" Sam hated that she'd had to give him up, but this was more important than just getting in trouble with your parents.

"He said they looked over Jared's room and the kitchen, the two areas they figured Tam was in the most. They didn't find a single clue of where he could be. They've interviewed his parents, but since they were at work all day and didn't know he was there, they aren't much help. That's why they went over to Tam's."

Another dead end. Sam wanted to scream. "Mom, is it okay if I call Jared? To see how it went with his parents?"

Mom nodded.

Sam dialed his number.

He answered on the second ring. "Hi, Sam."

"How'd it go?"

"Okay. I mean, my parents are upset, of course, but they aren't as mad as I thought they'd be. They're more concerned about Tam still being gone."

"Yeah, I understand." A thought occurred to her. "Hey, would it be okay if I came over and did an interview with you? I mean, your parents could be there and all. I just want to keep new information up on the paper's blog so people won't hesitate to call in if they hear from Tam."

"Hang on, let me ask my mom." A minute passed, then another before Jared came back on the line. "Yeah, my mom said it's fine. Your dad is over here anyway."

"Okay. I'll see you soon." Sam shoved her phone in her back pocket and went to her mother. "Mom, can you drive me over to Jared's house?" Quickly, she explained what she planned.

"Sure. You're driving yourself—and me—crazy here."

The drive to Chalamont Drive took less than ten minutes.

Sam and her mother had just joined Jared and his parents, as well as Sam's dad in the living room when Mrs. Hopkins touched her husband's shoulder. "Hey, turn up the volume," Mrs. Hopkins nodded to the television where Trevor Webster filled the screen again.

"Inside the Lee home, a phone has just rung. With our camera, we were able to see officers from the Pulaski County Sheriff's Office race into action. We have every reason to believe this call is from the missing child, Tam Lee." The reporter's voice trembled.

The camera panned to the front windows. A uniformed officer stood with a landline phone pressed against his ear. Mrs. Lee hovered next to him, her head close to the officer's.

"It's him," Sam's mother said, staring intently at the television.

"How can you tell?" Mr. Hopkins asked.

"Look at her face. She's hearing her son's voice. A mother knows these things." Sam's mother reached over and took Sam's hand and squeezed.

Sam's dad's cell phone rang. "Detective Sanderson."

Everyone stared at Sam's dad. He covered the mouthpiece of the phone and said, "It's the unit at the Lee house. They're having a hard time hearing him. Mrs. Lee has confirmed it's his voice, but they can't understand him. The connection is filled with static."

The other officer moved into camera range, his back to the front of the Lee house. "The activity in the Lee house is clearly—"

Mr. Hopkins pressed the mute button and silenced Trevor Webster.

"Wait. They've made out something he said," Sam's father spoke into the phone. "Stuck in a room? What does that mean?"

"Oh, mercy!" Mr. Hopkins leapt to his feet. "Let me check something."

Everyone sat still as Jared's dad rushed to his study.

"I've got him!" Mr. Hopkins hollered out after a minute or two.

Sam, her parents, and Jared and his mom rushed into the study. Tam leaned against Mr. Hopkins' desk.

"We have him! We've got Tam," Sam's father said into his phone. "He's okay."

Big tears burned Sam's eyes as she leaned over and hugged her mother.

"Yes, of course we'll stay with him until you get here." Sam's dad hung up the phone and looked at Tam. "Son, I'm sure you have a heck of a story to tell us, but your parents and the officers handling your case on their way, so maybe we should wait until they arrive for you to make a statement. Can we get you some water or anything?"

Tam shook his head, still not speaking.

"Charles, the media is at the Lee house. They know Tam called. They're going to follow them here," Sam's mother said.

Sam couldn't help herself . . . she ran over and gave Tam a big bear hug. "I was so worried about you," she whispered as she let him go, but took hold of his hand. She could see he was okay with her own eyes, but she needed to hold his hand to really accept her friend was safe. She didn't care what her father was saying about the media following Mr. and Mrs. Lee. All that mattered was that Tam had been found and he was okay.

Tam's hand squeezed hers back.

Thank You, God! Really, thanks for keeping Tam safe and letting him be found.

CHAPTER SEVENTEEN

Tam looked no worse for wear from his ordeal, but an explanation . . . well, the police weren't going to go away without an explanation. His mom and dad flanked him on both sides, his mother reaching over to hug him or hold his hand every few minutes.

Oh, a very detailed explanation was due.

Everyone was crowded into Jared's living room, waiting for the questioning to begin. Sam glanced around at the people in the room, taking note of who was present.

Tam and his parents, of course. They sat on one of the two couches in the living room. On the other couch sat Mr. Hopkins, then Jared and his mother. Deputies Jameson and Malone stood in front of the fireplace, with Sam's father and another officer sitting on the loveseat. Sam and her mother sat together on an oversized chair. Bella's dad, Mr. Kelly, stood in the corner.

The sheriff had let Mr. Kelly be present during the interview, but he had to agree to get approval from the sheriff's liaison officer before printing or running any story. Sam was just grateful she hadn't been asked to leave. She had a sneaking suspicion her mother had something to do with her being allowed to sit in on this.

"Now, young man, tell us everything, from start to finish," Deputy Jameson said to Tam.

Tam rolled the plastic water bottle in his hands, his face more than a little pale. "I'm in EAST, and while researching for my project about children's safety, I came across the information that most people believe the first twenty-four hours after a kid goes missing is the most critical. But that's actually inaccurate. It's the first three hours that are most critical, if a child's abductor isn't abducting them for money or to keep them."

Sam nodded. She'd been right. Tam had planned this for his project.

"I thought it would be a good idea to show what actually happens in the hours after a kid goes missing to show how much time can be wasted."

Deputy Jameson's frown deepened. "Like when law enforcement's time is wasted because a child fakes his own disappearance?"

Deputy Malone inched closer to Tam. "Go on. What was the point of that?"

"My point is that kids need to be more careful on their own. Sometimes their own actions or lack of awareness can prevent a tragedy from happening. But they have to know the signs. Know what to do. That's why I wanted to show how important it is to make these types of safety courses mandatory." Tam broke eye contact with Deputy Malone to look at Deputy Jameson. "I never intended to waste your time or anyone else's. Not like this."

"So, your intent was to prove to kids they need to be more aware . . . more careful . . ." Deputy Malone eased Tam back on track.

Sam thought Deputy Malone was one pretty cool cop. Not as cool as her dad or his partner, Buster Roscoe, but pretty cool.

"Right. So I did more research. I found that some kids are abducted by people they meet online. Often, people who misrepresent who they are."

"There are a lot of child predators out there," Sam's father said.

Tam nodded. "So I deliberately went onto a message board that I knew was considered dangerous and made a point to have conversations with several people who could be predators like that."

"How did you know the site was considered dangerous?" Deputy Jameson interrupted.

Tam's face reddened and he nodded, then stared at the floor. "Because I'm in charge of updating the recommended web sites on our school's blog that comes directly from law enforcement. We send a list of sites kids tell us about to the police and they send back their recommendations. The one I went onto was flagged as dangerous."

Sam nodded to herself. She'd been so right about her friend.

Tam took a sip of water, licking his lips. Sam could only imagine how nervous he must be right now, but his mother's constant patting of his arm probably helped him a lot. Tam continued. "Anyway, I used my own computer because I knew the police would go through it, trace my history, and see the conversation. It would take time to see there was no connection between my conversation and my disappearance."

"Wasting the time and resources of law enforcement," Deputy Jameson grumbled.

Tam's face reddened again and he shifted on the couch. Sam felt sorry for him—she knew how it felt to have Deputy Jameson angry. Then again, Sam considered, she'd spent a lot of energy being upset that the police thought Tam had run away. In actuality, he kind of had. She felt a rub against her conscience. Maybe she shouldn't get annoyed so easily. Maybe the police did know how to run an investigation. Yeah, she knew that, but sometimes . . .

"Why don't you tell your story the way you executed everything, okay?" Deputy Malone said to Tam, but cast a look at his partner.

"Okay." Tam let out a long breath and met Sam's stare. "My project is about how kids need to be more careful in their actions on the Internet and elsewhere."

The room was silent, except for Mrs. Lee's occasional sniffles.

"Through my research, I learned that law enforcement looks first, if there isn't a custodial issue, to see if the child is a possible runaway. I knew my dad's rules and I knew he wouldn't bend them without good reason. I deliberately made a point of posting on Facebook that I was having a disagreement with my father about his rules." Tam looked at his dad, his eyes wide. "I'm sorry, Dad. I didn't mean to paint you in a bad light, but I needed to publicly show just enough reason for the police to think I might have been upset enough to run away."

Tam's dad didn't look very impressed. Okay, Sam admitted, he looked angry, and Tam's explanation apparently wasn't improving Mr. Lee's mood at all.

Tam rolled the water bottle in his hands again. "I knew that would be enough to lay the groundwork for the police to initially consider me a runaway. That would start the three hours that are most critical in abductions committed by people who mean to harm the child."

Deputy Malone nodded, encouraging Tam to continue.

"I had already set up the message board scenario in

the event my parents were able to convince the police I wasn't a runaway. I knew the first things they'd look at would be my computer and cell phone, which I had left at home because I didn't want the police to use the built-in GPS to track me."

Tam paused to take a drink of water. Sam's stare collided with his. He gave her a slight smile, then straightened and set down the bottle. "I'd already worked it out with Jared to let me stay at his house." He glanced at Jared. "I really didn't mean to get anybody in trouble. I'm so sorry."

Jared shrugged.

"Your plan?" Deputy Jameson snapped.

"Right." Tam nodded. "Since I'd already made the arrangements with Jared, I wanted to leave another red herring for the police, so I asked Jared to put a note in my locker that said everything was set for the morning."

The tension could have been sliced in the room like a loaf of bread.

"Please try to remember I didn't plan to really be missing. I even had a backup plan in case something went wrong."

"How'd that work out for you?" Deputy Jameson said, wearing a sneer.

Sam wanted to stick her tongue out at him, but figured her mom and dad both would make her leave if she did. She was supposed to be mature.

"Well, not very well. I guess, in hindsight, I should've

used a different backup plan. Or had a backup for the backup."

"What was your backup?" Sam asked.

Four different officers stared at her, as if they'd forgotten she was there.

But Tam answered her question, which explained another lead. "I had deleted all my notes and research out of my project files in EAST in case anyone went looking. I didn't want anyone to find anything about my project."

"I know. I could only find some of your research notes in Mrs. Shine's documents," Sam blurted out.

Tam's eyes widened. "I didn't even think about her notes on my project."

Deputy Malone cleared his throat. "Could we please get back to your telling of the story?"

"Sorry," Sam muttered, then dropped her gaze to the floor.

"I'd cleared my files, but had them all saved to a jump drive. I had made plans to meet with someone before school on Wednesday and give her the drive with instructions to take it to Mrs. Shine after school."

"Darby French, right?" Deputy Malone asked.

Tam nodded. "We had planned to meet before school on the side of the building, so no one would see me and report that I'd been there that morning. Only, she didn't show up. I don't know what happened, but Jared got there and I had to leave with him to get into his house." Tam stared at Mr. and Mrs. Hopkins. "Again, I'm very sorry."

Neither of the Hopkins said a word. The awkward silence was deafening.

"Anyway, I came here. Jared was very clear that I needed to pick up after myself, not to make a mess or break anything." Tam took another drink of water. "I did my best to do just that. I read, I watched a little television, but then I worried that there might be a timer on the satellite or something and I didn't want to get Jared in trouble, so I started wandering around the house."

Tam shifted in his chair stuffed between his parents, looking uncomfortable.

"I went into Mr. Hopkin's study since the door was open. I thought about checking my email, but realized that would be a very bad idea. Then I saw the geometric sculpture." He glanced at Mr. Hopkins. "I just wanted to look more closely at it, and I promise I was very, very careful with it." He licked his lips. "As soon as I picked it up, the bookcase broke away and revealed a hidden room!"

Sam's pulse kicked up a notch as if she was finding a secret room too.

"I carefully set the sculpture down and stepped cautiously into the room." Tam took another drink of water. His Adam's apple bobbed as he swallowed. Loudly.

Or maybe it just seemed loud because everyone was so quiet, hanging on Tam's every word.

"It's the coolest thing ever. At first I thought it was the coolest storm shelter I'd ever seen, including anything I'd ever seen on television. I saw the bathroom and all the supplies and I remember thinking this was more than just a storm shelter. I couldn't imagine someone needing so much food, water, and blankets and stuff just to tough out a storm."

Sam caught her mother taking notes on her tablet. Mr. Kelly was recording the conversation with his little voice-activated digital recorder. It prompted Sam to check her phone to make sure it was still recording. It was.

"Then I thought maybe it was like a survivalist room. I've seen those on different movies and television shows and they have a lot of supplies. But then I realized the room wasn't really big enough and while there was plenty of food and water for about a week for one person, it wouldn't last more than a day or two for a family of three."

Sam snuck a glance at Mr. Hopkins. His face was as red as a fire truck, his puffy cheeks looking like he would blow at any given minute.

"So that's when I figured it wasn't just a storm shelter, but a panic room. I'd definitely seen a movie about one of those, and that made me wonder if there were closed circuit TVs and computers like the one I saw on television."

Sam remembered that movie. She'd watched it with her dad a long time ago. It was about a woman and her daughter who locked themselves in the panic room when some robbers came. The plot stuck with Sam because Dad had used the opportunity to tell her what she should do at their house in the event someone broke in.

Tam continued, "I figured since I hadn't been able to give the jump drive to Darby, I would set my email to send it as an attachment and schedule the delivery to go to Mrs. Shine after five. I knew as soon as she read everything, she'd call the police and my parents." His mother sniffled and hugged him again.

Tam straightened on the couch. "As soon as I booted up the computer in the panic room, it asked for the passcode. I typed in a string in an attempt to bypass the security code, but all of a sudden, the whole system froze and the door to the room automatically shut."

Sam sucked in air. She would've freaked out.

"I tried to get it to stop, but nothing I pressed on the computer would work. Once the door shut, I knew I was stuck. I heard the bolts in the cement slide. I knew."

"It's a fail safe," Mr. Hopkins said. "Against intruders. If the thumbprint isn't activated on the computer within fifteen seconds of the computer being pulled out of sleep mode, the fail safe automatically closes and seals the door so you can't open it from the inside. It must be opened from the outside." He glared at Tam. "It's to prevent interlopers."

"It works, sir. Scariest sound in the world is that door closing and locking." Tam's face was white.

"That is its purpose." Mr. Hopkins was clearly not open to cutting Tam any slack.

Sam looked at Jared. He, too, was a little pale. Neither of his parents had so much as cracked a half-smile that Sam had seen the whole time she'd been at their home. She felt sorry for him . . . and Tam. She recognized that look both fathers wore, had seen it on her own father's face many times. Serious repercussions would be forthcoming.

Yep, Sam felt very sorry for Tam and Jared indeed.

CHAPTER EIGHTEEN

"So, you were locked in?" Deputy Malone put the interview back on track.

Tam nodded. "I wasn't too worried at first. I knew there had to be Internet going into the room, so figured I'd just work to bypass the computer's issue and get online. I could either email Jared or use a chat program to get in touch with him. Even if I were stuck in the room until school got out, that'd be okay, because Jared could get me out."

Sam was right—Tam was scary brilliant.

"I didn't realize he had no idea the room was even there," Tam said.

Sam chanced a look at Mr. Hopkins. By the look on Mrs. Hopkins' face, Sam would bet that she hadn't known about the room either.

She was sure glad she wouldn't be at the Hopkins house tonight when the crowd cleared.

"Understand that once my plan went sideways, I was still working on how to get around it. Even if I'd chatted with or emailed Jared and he didn't know what I was talking about, I could have told him and he would have gone to his dad and his dad would've let me out. I wasn't concerned because I figured that would be the worst case scenario. I didn't want to get Jared in trouble, but either way, I'd still get out before ten."

Tam took another drink of water. "If Jared had to have his dad get me out, then my plan would be seriously disrupted, but I would've still had the proof that in the initial time after a child goes missing, law enforcement has to go through preliminary measures that could . . . well, it could just take up precious time."

Sam did the mental calculations. Tam was reported missing by four fifteen. If Jared's dad didn't get home until five thirty and then didn't get Tam out until six before they called Mr. and Mrs. Lee, it'd be close to the crucial initial three hours.

"It took me a couple of hours, but I made some pretty good headway on the computer. I'd gotten it stripped down to code and was just about to start creating some crawlers that would help me find the Internet connections when the tornado sirens went off. Man, the speakers in that room amplified the sirens. I thought my head would explode."

Mr. Hopkins grimaced. "It's a feature of the room. In the event any alert such as an Emergency Broadcast System alert or the tornado sirens go off, the system will play at high volume inside the room."

"It's crazy loud," Tam confirmed.

"And you didn't hear this?" Deputy Jameson asked Mr. Hopkins.

"The room is soundproof. You can't hear anything that goes on in that room." Mr. Hopkins looked away.

"So, um." Tam took another drink of water. His bottle was below the halfway mark now. "It scared me, but then I remembered I was in a very safe place to ride out a tornado. I was safer than if I were at home or at school."

"The room is designed to withstand an F-five tornado and even up to three hundred and thirty mile per hour winds," Mr. Hopkins said, the first semblance of something akin to a smile on his face.

"So it's a storm shelter?" Sam's father asked.

Mr. Hopkins shrugged. "Of sorts. It was here when we bought the house, put in by the builder because he was paranoid of being a victim of a home invasion."

"I remember the realtor telling us about it, but I don't remember seeing it," Mrs. Hopkins ventured.

"It was after we closed on the house that he showed me." But Mr. Hopkins turned as red as Tam had been earlier.

Sam was *really* glad she wouldn't be at the Hopkins home once Jared's parents were alone.

"Continue, please, Tam," Deputy Malone said.

"I had food and water and a bathroom. I was safe. So I didn't panic at all," Tam said. "Until the power went out."

Sam squirmed uncomfortably in the chair she shared with her mother, just imagining what it would feel like to be trapped in a room, all alone, tornado sirens going off, and then to lose electricity. Yep, she'd freak out big time.

"It was pitch black in there and that normally wouldn't bother me, but then I realized there may not be a backup ventilation system in place in the event of a power outage. That scared me more than a possible tornado."

Oh, yeah, Sam would be having one of those hissy fits Makayla's always talking about.

"But the power was only out for about thirty minutes or so before it came back on. When I heard the ventilation system kick back on, let me tell you, I let out a big sigh of relief on that one, that's for sure." Tam smiled.

No one smiled back.

"So I started to get back to the computer and that's when I realized the Internet connection was gone. I figured it was probably like some of the servers at school—if the server goes down, it needs to be manually restarted." Tam looked at Mr. Hopkins. "In case you didn't know that about your feed into that room, that's how yours is set up. I'd recommend you get a dedicated server strictly for that room."

Mr. Hopkins' cheeks puffed out again.

"The Internet was gone?" Deputy Malone asked.

Tam nodded. "I knew there wasn't a chance to get it back unless I could get out. So, I started searching for another way to make contact. I went through all the supply boxes in there. Plenty of food, batteries, flashlights, heat packs, and fans, but not a single emergency cell phone." Tam looked at Mr. Hopkins again. "Something else you should consider stocking your room with."

"There's a phone hidden in a secret panel in the floor of the room," Mr. Hopkins snarled. "People who are authorized to be in the room know how to access the phone."

"Well, I didn't." Tam drained his water bottle, not looking as nervous as before. Then again, he was probably exhausted and ready to go home and get some sleep. "I pretty much realized I was stuck there until someone let me out. I figured someone would check the room when they came home and realized the power had been off. But no one did."

Silence filled the room once again, but this time, the air felt different. Not as much animosity, but more of everyone lost in their own thoughts about being trapped with no one coming to the rescue.

Sam wouldn't have made it, not that many days. She

was sure she'd still be curled up in a little ball, probably crying for her mom.

"After a couple of days, I knew no one was going to open that room unless they had reason to. That's when I figured I had to do something." Tam's voice shook a little. "I decided that I would find the electrical wires and cross them until a fire started. I knew the house had an alarm system, because Jared had to turn it off for me to stay there, and I'd seen the panel. There was a fire monitoring and a carbon monoxide monitoring service."

"You tried to set my house on fire?" Jared asked, his eyes wide.

"I didn't want to, but man, I was stuck. I'd been in there two nights and three days with no way out in sight. I didn't know about the phone, so I didn't know I had a choice."

"But if you set an electrical fire, wouldn't that have been in the room where you were?" Sam blurted out. When everyone turned to stare at her, she covered her mouth with her hand.

Tam answered anyway. "It was a calculated risk. I'd found the fire extinguisher, so I knew if it became too dangerous I could put it out. I was hoping that the fire would cause smoke to go through the house's ventilation system or something and register enough for the alarm company to get the code of a fire and send someone."

"Most likely, that would have worked," Deputy Malone said. "I have the same alarm system, and even electrical fires send the alarm straight to the fire department."

"But I didn't need to do that," Tam said. "When I traced the wiring, I found a box with exchanges. In there, I found a phone line that was hooked up. All I had to do was splice into it, find something I could use to dial, and something to use as a mouthpiece."

Sam stared at Tam, amazed at her friend. No way would she have been able to do all that. Maybe she wasn't as smart and independent as she thought.

"It took me some time, but I found an old coax splitter and was able to—" Tam glanced around the room. "I was able to make a call. The first time, I was so excited the call actually went through that I didn't have the interface secured. I was barely able to get my name out before the wires crossed and I lost the call."

Sam caught her mother's eye and smiled. At least she didn't have to go down the dark and scary path.

"I took my time and spliced it up better, but it took me some time because I didn't have any electrical tape. If anything touched the exposed wires, the call would be dropped. I used a bandage and the first aid tape from the first aid kit to secure it as best I could." Tam gave a little smile. "I guess it was good enough because I was finally able to get the call out. The next thing I knew, the door opened and I was free."

●●●

"I still can't believe it all. It's crazy," Makayla said.

Sam adjusted her Bluetooth headset and laid back on her bed, petting Chewy who lay beside her, much to BabyKitty's great disappointment. "I know. Tam's dad was furious, even though his mother said she was proud of her son's bravery and ingenuity."

"What about Jared?"

Sam grinned even though her best friend couldn't see it over the phone. "I imagine things are quite strained at the Hopkins household, but Jared might be saved. It was pretty clear Mr. Hopkins had the room and neither Jared nor his mother knew anything about it. They moved in a couple of years ago. From what I heard—"

"You mean eavesdropped?"

"Whatever. Mr. Hopkins said he'd practically forgotten about the room. I don't know about that, because the room was part of the alarm system and was fully stocked, but I think their being at odds helps Jared stay out of the hot seat."

"I can't imagine having a room like that in my house and not telling my husband," Makayla said.

"Oh, when did you go get married and not tell me?"

"Stop." Makayla laughed. "Seriously, do you think your dad would have a secret room that your mom didn't know about?"

"Nope, but just to be safe, I asked them both if we have a panic room in our house. They assured me we don't, which is kind of a bummer because it's really cool."

"Have you written up your last article yet?" Makayla asked.

"No. I just don't know what to write yet." She sat up on the bed. "And guess what?"

"What?"

"Dad told me they caught *tutorcool*. One of the kids he tried to kidnap picked him out of a lineup. Dad said he should plead guilty and will be going to jail for a long time." That made Sam feel much safer somehow.

"That's great news."

"Yeah. And because of Mr. Kelly's report, two area senators are talking with Tam about his project goal to get mandatory safety education programs in the public schools."

"That's pretty awesome," Mac said.

"Yeah, so something else I'll add to my article."

"Okay, my turn. Guess what?" asked Makayla.

"What?" Sam rolled onto her side and propped her head on her hand.

"I talked to my mom about the whole lawyer thing."

"How'd that go?"

"She said that it's okay if I don't know what I want to be right now."

"See," Sam said. "I told you."

"She said she would rather I wait and see what God's plan is for me rather than just jumping ahead with my own ideas."

"Cool. So hey, I'm gonna go and get my article written so I can get Mom to help me start laying out stuff to pack," Sam said.

"I'm still so jelly. Are you still coming to my karate tournament tomorrow?"

"Of course. Mom's bringing her camera too."

"Oh, man. Okay, later."

Sam tossed the headset onto the desk and moved to sit in front of her computer. She opened the program to write the post. Her fingers sat still on the keyboard for a handful of minutes, until she thought through everything she'd learned again. Most importantly, to do what is necessary to learn how to keep safe. Yes, God was always in control, but learning how to be safe was just smart.

—While the staff of the *Senator Speak* is very happy to have our own Tam Lee back safe and accounted for, it is this reporter's opinion that we should all make the effort to take care. Take care to be aware of our surroundings. Take care to abide by rules set by our parents. (Yes, even the ones we think are lame.) Take care to tell the people who matter to us that they do. And to take care to put people first . . . not just a project or a promotion or a story. Because in the end, it's the connections you have in your brief time on earth that matter. Sound Off, Senators, and take care. ~Sam Sanderson, reporting

EPILOGUE

"Welcome back to Galveston, Texas," Sam's dad said, the hint of sunburn from a few days ago already turned to a nice tan.

"Oh, I don't want to get off the ship," Sam's mother replied. "Can we just pretend we're back in the Caribbean? Please."

"I want to be back in Dolphin Cove, swimming with Darwin." Sam would never, ever forget how amazing it was to swim with the rescued dolphin. She couldn't wait to show Makayla all the pictures she'd taken of the cruise.

Grand Cayman and Cozumel . . . it'd been wonderful. Sam decided she loved cruising. The ship itself was amazing, with the coolest restaurants, twenty-four hour pizza and ice cream, and two giant waterslides. They'd been on the second deck in a balcony room, where she could sit outside every night and listen to the waves. Some nights, she could even feel the spray of the water on her face when she stood at the rail.

Speaking of Makayla . . .

"Are we docked yet?"

"Yep. As of about fifteen or twenty minutes ago," Dad answered.

"So we aren't in international waters anymore? I can use my cell?" She'd been quite upset when she learned she wouldn't be able to use her phone because of the outrageous charges. Mom had locked all their phones in the in-cabin safe until that morning.

Her mother sighed and laid her head back in the chair. "We're officially back home. The child is ready to be on her phone."

Dad laughed, leaned over, and kissed Mom. Right on the mouth. Eww. "I bet I know someone else whose fingers are itching to check her email and see what assignments she has lined up," he teased.

"So, can I?" Sam pushed.

"Yes. Go ahead," Dad said.

She quickly turned her phone off airplane mode. The phone acted like it was possessed. It vibrated and dinged for a good three minutes solid. Sam began scrolling through her messages. Her breath caught as she read the last one from her best friend.

> Sam, call as soon as you get this message. Felicia called, and Aubrey Damas has quit the paper. Felicia says she's pretty sure Ms. Pape is going to give the editor's job to you. CALL ME.

Sam sat in stunned silence.

A minute passed.

Two.

Three.

A slow smile made its way across her face.

So this is what it felt like to have a dream come true.

FINALLY!

DISCUSSION QUESTIONS

1. Sam uses her talents as a writer and reporter and her natural God-given ability to evaluate situations to help people whenever she can. Describe how she helped in this situation? Are there times when trying to be helpful can also be a hindrance? Explain how that could happen.
2. The disappearance of a child is a very serious situation and never to be taken lightly. Do you think the law enforcement officers tried to dissuade Sam because they didn't think she could possibly be of help? Why were they hesitant to take her seriously in their investigation?
3. Deputies Malone and Jameson had differing attitudes about the value of Sam's theories and thoughts about Tam's disappearance. Why was that?
4. Sam's father has an incredible sense of right and wrong and fairness in how he deals with everyone, from Sam to the Lees to the deputies in charge of the case. How do people develop a strong fortitude? Where does that come from?
5. Computers and other electronic devices are amazing machines that serve us well in many cases. But there are times that they can introduce dangers into our

lives. How were electronics a good and a bad thing in *Without a Trace*?

6. Tam took a risk to prove a point. Have you ever done something you probably shouldn't have, just to make a point? What happened? Discuss ways you can get your point across in a safe manner.
7. Sam's friend Makayla hesitates to break the rules, even as Sam tries to convince her that it is in Tam's best interest? Have you ever had your beliefs, your convictions, questioned? Did you stick up for yourself and stay true to what you believe? Or did you allow yourself to be persuaded to do something other than your original plan?
8. Sam just knew that Tam wouldn't have run off without good reason because of his reputation ... his past behavior backed up her strong conviction. What do you think people see as your reputation? What would you like to be your reputation? Discuss ways you can act to support that reputation.
9. Have you ever felt so sure about something that you were willing to risk trouble with parents, teachers, and other adults to prove your point or theory? What happened? How can young people ensure that their ideas and thoughts are taken seriously by others?
10. Mr. and Mrs. Lee were very worried about their son. What does the Bible tell us about worrying? Discuss Matthew 6:27.

11. Sam knows that prayer is a powerful tool at all times. When does she use prayer in this situation? How does it bring comfort and peace to a difficult time?
12. Tam wanted to stress how important it was to realize God was always in control, but also wanted kids to learn how to be safe. What are things you can do to keep yourself safe at school? On the internet?
13. Do a little research. What exactly is an Amber Alert? How are they effective?
14. The panic room was pretty cool. Discuss some reasons to go into a panic room. Would you be scared if you'd gotten locked inside like Tam? Discuss what you would have done.
15. There are unfortunately many cases of children having trouble in our world today—from disappearances to getting hurt or injured or suffering in natural disasters. What are some Bible verses that could be used to help bring comfort to families experiencing troubles with their children?

ACKNOWLEDGMENTS

I owe a huge amount of gratitude to the whole team at Zonderkidz for helping the Samantha Sanderson series see the light of day. I truly appreciate each of you for extending your talent and skill on my behalf, especially Mary Hassinger. You've been such an awesome editor to work with.

My most humble gratitude to amazing author, Ronie Kendig, who helped me work out this plot when my back was against the wall. You rock!

Special thanks to Robinson Middle School who let me share how special they are with the rest of the world. I played around with possibilities and lay of the land as I saw fit. Any mistakes in the representation of details are mine, which I twisted in the best interest of my story.

My most sincere thanks to my awesome agent, Steve Laube (HP), who not only is an amazing agent, but makes me laugh when I get too serious. THANK YOU.

Thank you for ALWAYS being in my corner: Mom, Bubba and Lisa, Brandon, Rachel, and especially my Papa, who I love and miss every day.

I couldn't do what I do without my girls—Emily Carol, Remington Case, and Isabella Co-Ceaux. I love each of you so much! Thank y'all so much for your support and encouragement when I needed to write. And my precious grandsons, Benton and Zayden. You are joys in my life.

I'm blessed to have such an amazing husband who puts up with my craziness, but also is a great brainstorm partner and research assistant. You amaze me with your insight and your love and support. I love you with everything I have.

Finally, all glory to my Lord and Savior, Jesus Christ. I can do all things through Him who gives me strength.

Samantha Sanderson

Written by Robin Caroll

Samantha Sanderson
At the Movies

Samantha Sanderson
On the Scene

Samantha Sanderson
Off the Record

Samantha Sanderson
Without a Trace

The Samantha Sanderson Series introduces us to Sam Sanderson, an independent, resourceful, future award-winning journalist and her best friend Makayla. The two 7th graders enjoy shopping, texting, going to the mall and the skating rink—and sniffing out the next big mysteries to report in the school paper.

Available in stores and online!